REBIRTHS

REBIRTHS

DENVOR FERNANDEZ

PARTRIDGE
A Penguin Random House Company

Fern Dale, Ummini, Dhoni P.O.
Palakkad-678009, Kerala e-mail-denvorfern@yahoo.co.in
Ph.no: 0491-2557121, 09400419921

ISBN:	Hardcover	978-1-4828-1717-1
	Softcover	978-1-4828-1718-8
	Ebook	978-1-4828-1728-7

To order additional copies of this book, contact
Partridge India
000 800 10062 62
www.partridgepublishing.com/india
orders.india@partridgepublishing.com

INVOCATION

God! I love you. My words, actions and inactions are nothing but gifts to you. My mistakes are for your entertainment. My flaws and ignorant passions stand only as a foil to your perfection, that can not be comprehended by human reason. My knowledge and wisdom will lose its grandeur the moment I touch your infinite being. The strength of my love will break as a twig the moment I experience your love. Let your spirit enter through this work of art. Please forgive my sins, which I have made in this work directly or indirectly, as I have forgiven the readers who are going to criticise me. I have a human mind and body. The ideas that I produce may suffer from its stains. Both my strengths and weaknesses can become the instruments of sin. Teach me to love you with all my strength. Teach me to love my fellow humans. I know very well that whenever one deviates from the path of love he or she sins. Sometimes our weaker feelings make us to do that. My knowledge is nothing but a drop of tear in the ocean of melancholy. Forgive my lack of knowledge. Let not pride, ego and fame haunt me the way it can haunt writers and thinkers. Let not lust and the other passions of the body blind me. Do not let me get addicted to my own work but let me discover the true essence of it, if there is any.

God! Bless my readers! Let not the false emotions, feelings and passions in my work blind them. This work is also a gift for them. Teach them to laugh at my mistakes and judge me rightly. Fill them with joy and love and let it overflow unto others. God! Do not let Dominic know about it.

PROLOGUE

In the year 12200 BC, a sage was waiting with patience and earnestness to teach about the divine knowledge to anyone who dared to ask. He did not wait for long as many disciples thronged into his humble abode. Most of them were those got attracted to the fact that knowledge is the key to power and wealth. Of course, there were exceptions; sages love exceptions. He once said, 'Those who have come here expecting to lust after power and wealth please leave this holy place and prepare for your journey to hell.' Many pupils left disappointing the sage; he regretted his words. Soon, he realized that his regret stemmed from the truth that he himself felt powerful being the guru of thousands and earning a decent fortune. The few who stayed back changed the history of the world.

Karma, a seven-year-old child prodigy, was his most faithful disciple. Karma was more interested in the divine mantras and chants which could give humans the wisdom of the Gods. Karma loved the gods so much that he wanted to become like them; he wanted to be the lonely One, the blissful One, the silent One.

'Son, it is not child's play. You have to spend years in the wilderness meditating and praying to the Gods along with the severe penances,' the sage told Karma. The sage wanted Karma to become a world-renowned teacher who would found his own religion and not a lonely hermit.

The young boy left his school and meditated in the forest. He gave all his wealth to the poor. He gave up the protection and dignity of man-made clothes. He stood on burning woods during the hot summers and took repeated dips in ice-cold streams during winters. He never forgot the chants and mantras that praised the gods. Leaves and roots became his food. His muscular body shrank.

The gods were shocked at Karma's penance. Indra, the god of thunder, said, 'If Karma goes on with his penance we will have to lend him the divine mantras which were hidden from humankind for millions of years. We have to pass on those divine mantras that make gods Gods.'

'You have to do that.' ordered the voice of the Supreme-Soul, the God of Gods.

'I am the only true God. The Creator, the Preserver and the Destroyer are nothing but my costumes. I am the Beginning, the Middle and the End.' said the voice of the Supreme-Soul. 'When I created humankind I poured out something of Me into them. I reside within them. I am part of them and they are parts of Me. Nothing is lost and nothing is gained since everything happens within Me. You are free to do anything with Karma but make sure you do not touch his mind and his soul.'

Ten years later, on a winter morn, Karma looked at his body and was surprised to see his body filled with flesh and vitality. His praised the gods but did not stop his penance. All of a sudden, Karma started to feel very thirsty. 'Sir, Would you like to drink some water?' said a young girl with a pot filled with water. Karma kept quite. 'Sir, Can I take you home?' asked the girl, 'My father is looking for a boy to get me married. I want you to be that boy.' Karma was sexually attracted towards the girl. 'No,' said Karma politely, 'You will find a better husband'. Karma did not let his sexual desires to conquer over his body for the world was death and the heavens life.

A beautiful princess camped in the forest along with her maidservants. On seeing Karma, she was infatuated. 'These are my maids and these are my riches; they are all yours if you wish to marry me.' said the princess. Karma politely refused. She and her maids tried all tricks to seduce Karma but all to no avail. When her false ego got badly hurt, she made the king's soldiers capture Karma.

'I can't marry your daughter. I do not belong to your world. May your daughter find a better husband!' said Karma politely to the king. The princess killed herself. Karma continued his penance in jail. No royal torture could shatter his patience.

The day Karma got his first gray hair God appeared before him. Karma requested God to teach him the mantra of immortality. God politely refused and promised to teach him the mantra of rebirths instead. Whoever hears the mantra will remember every incident that its previous bodies experienced. An echo was born in Karma's ears. Karma remembered the times he was in planet Dei. His soul had worn three strange bodies before it came into his. He had traveled in flying chariots. He was tortured in strange ways. He gave birth to young ones. He had spoken to his loved ones twenty thousand light years away from earth. He could replicate himself. He had had the knowledge to control the minds of others. He could create slaves with the elements of nature. He remembered how planet Dei was destroyed. Its greedy inhabitants converted Dei into a treeless desert.

Karma was the most knowledgeable person on earth. He married the king's second daughter, who was born to the king's eighteenth wife ten years after karma's arrest; he had children. He told the stories and adventures of his previous births to put his children to sleep. Before his death, he taught the mantra of rebirths to his eldest son and said 'A knowledgeable man is one who knows many things about the world around him but only a few things about his being. A man of wisdom is one who knows more about himself than the things around him for inside him resides a soul, which is a piece fallen from the soul of God. This mantra will make you a man of wisdom'. The eldest son taught it to his favourite wife who told it to her lover. The lover told it to his loved ones. The lover told it to an enemy who changed his mind after the wisdom of three births got into him. Some got mad after knowing about their past lives and shouted the mantra in public. The mantra made people wise in a strange way. A man called Newton read the mantra aloud from a book of alchemy. He used his knowledge to become famous as a scientist. Shakespeare heard the mantra from a deer hunter and used his knowledge to write plays and poems. In his previous birth Shakespeare was a bisexual who was torn between the love of a black woman and an Indian prince.

The mantra was the greatest secret ever kept. The mantra was the greatest thing responsible for the evolution of humankind. It preserved the human tradition and culture for years.

'Karma, you have sinned,' said the sage to the desert air, 'the young girl with the pot was the Supreme God, the Creator of all creators. I lived for two hundred years just to preserve my disciple's sin.' The sage died but the desert echoed his words for eternity.

1

When Dominic opened his eyes, he remembered everything that happened in his past three lives. The astrologer who promised him nirvana had vanished. Dominic got up; he felt the cramps in his legs bothering him. He took a deep breath and all the feelings of his body were pushed into nadir. The wild roars of the Chennai traffic could not interrupt the peaceful silence that was flowing through his mind. The scorching heat, which would penetrate the hardest of skins, could not touch him. The wayside garbage, which stared impolitely at every passerby, did not insult him. He took out his purse to take out his ID card. The one thousand rupee note that was taken from the ATM to pay the examination fee was missing from his purse. He was not unhappy. In a few months, he was going to leave Assisi—the college he loved and hated.

'Hello, Mom'

'The money is missing.'

'Yes'

'I don't know.'

'Hmm . . .'

'I am really sorry'

'Ok'

'Ok'

'Thank you, ma'

2

Francis Rodrigues said proudly 'This is my son Dominic Rodrigues. He is planning to join here to do his MA in English literature from this college. We have heard that Assisi College is one of the best colleges in this locality; is it true? My son scored seventy-five percent in his BA. So, your son is going for MSW.'

He was not listening to what the other man replied; he was lost in thoughts about his son. He had a perfect plan for him and his imagination conspired with his wish for a happy life to see into the future of things.

Fathers dream of immortality through the eyes of their sons; fathers mould their sons into their own images. 'Think like me, walk like me, live like me and die like me.' They whisper to their sons without actually saying anything. There begins their tragedy. Dominic played Adam to his father's God. That was his tragedy.

3

Professor Simon drank a sip of coffee and asked 'So . . . Dominic Rodrigues Application number 15 . . . Do you know anything about D H Lawrence?'

'Yes. He wrote books like Sons and Lovers, Lady Chatterley's . . .'

'Who is your favourite author?'

'Sidney Sheldon'

'Oh! That is pulp fiction.'

'He is . . .'

'Thank you'

Dominic looked at his name in the notice board after a few hours:

Entrance test marks: 45/50, Interview: 29/50. SELECTED.

4

Hallowing, hallowing little moon

How I wonder what you are?

Up above the world so high

Like a condom in the sky. (Written in my friend's notebook)

—Dominic Rodrigues

27.07.2008, Chennai

5

'You know famous people like Hari Nair and Gobind Sing studied in Assisi College' said Justine. Shabri replied 'Did you read in the papers about a youngster who was arrested for rape in Bangalore? Well, he studied in Assisi College'. Justine thought very high about the institution and the management and could not think about the college as anything lesser that the dome of the temple over mount Olympus.

'Making boys and girls sit in separate rows is a form of sexual discrimination; do you think so, Dominic?' asked Shabri to make Justine frown.

Dominic knew that it was better to pass the ball with a few seconds of silence.

'Those are rules which we have to follow for our own good. A rapist rapes because of his will to dominate over the opposite sex. His destructive ego and his burning lust make him do it. Rules teach us self-control.' replied Justine.

'Well, that leads to a kind of gap in our sexually repressed minds which later will make us rapists and criminals. Why can't the rapist be a 'she' instead of a 'he'?'

'Shut up, Shabri'

'Fuck you!'

Shabri made his trademark display of his middle finger.

6

Dominic felt lonely. His roommates had just gone for an international Physics conference. Dominic was happy in his loneliness. Dominic could not get space to masturbate for nearly two weeks. Boys who had six-packs always surrounded him. Shah Rukh Khan in Om Shanthi Om inspired them. Dominic let his imagination wander. The phone sang; Dominic picked it up.

'Hello Dominic. This is your uncle James.'

'Uncle James! Where were you for the past ten years? You left us without a word. My Mom said you died in an old age home in Kunnur.'

'I am in Chennai. I want to tell you a secret.'

Dominic met Uncle James at Chennai Beach railway station. Dominic used to go there in order to buy movie DVDs. His uncle looked old with a long white hair and a goat beard. 'Come!' said Uncle James and took Dominic to his house in Anna Nagar in an old-fashioned cycle.

'I have a lab in the basement. No one here knows that I am a scientist. You should preserve my legacy.' said Uncle James bluntly.

Uncle James took Dominic to his basement and showed him a big machine. 'This is a teleportation machine. This will help you to travel to other planets.' Dominic had many questions in his mind, 'How does this machine work? Is there life in other planets? Is it safe to travel in such a machine?'

'You sent pictures to your friends with your mobile phone, do you? Each colour and each segment of the picture file will have a code. These codes will reach your friend's mobile phone and will be decoded. Your friend gets the picture. Likewise, all the cells in your body will be decoded and recoded in a planet 5000 light years away. Yes, there is life in other planets. I am going to sent you to planet Zod. All the information you need is there in this backpack.' So saying Uncle James made Dominic wear a heavy backpack, gave him an injection and put him in a pyramidal shaped glass case that was connected to the machine. Green laser lights moved inside the glass case as if it was scanning something. 'Good luck!' said Uncle James.

Dominic found his body parts disintegrating. The grass was long, thick and wet. Dominic looked around. 'My God, I am in Zod.' he thought. He opened his backpack to find small books and weird looking electronic gadgets. He took out the book titled 'Read me first' and started reading.

"Dear Dominic,

Hope you have watched all the films of your favourite director Steven Spielberg. You imagine of alien creatures with big heads and small bodies like the visual effects technicians show us. Well, that is not what you are going to see. You can breathe the air. Zod is filled with oxygen. So, take a deep breath. Humans—Homo sapiens surround you! Zod has an environment similar to that of earth. Zod is not technologically advanced as Earth but is dominated by humans. The humans in the planet are facing extinction because a fatal virus has killed all the male members. The injection I gave you prevents this prostrate gland-affecting virus to enter into your body. It is up to you to pour life into this planet. Good luck!'

When Dominic closed the book, he heard a splash. He turned around to find a pool filled with fresh water. A half a dozen of young women were bathing in the pond. After their bath, they dressed themselves in clothes made of jasmine flowers and thin green twigs.

Dominic heard a sound behind him.

'Kuvaka!'

He turned back and saw a young girl looking at him with astonishment. A bevy of angry women tied him up and took him to the village court.

Two similar looking middle-aged women were shouting orders to other women. They sat on wooden chairs and wore crowns made of gold.

'Teli-wa-miko?' They asked Dominic. Dominic did not answer.

The two women shouted in their highest pitch 'Teli-wa-miko?'

Dominic shivered. An arrow from nowhere pierced Dominic's arm. Dominic felt sleepy and fainted.

When Dominic woke up, he found himself in a very wide muddy well. Plants bearing strange fruits were hanging from the walls of the well. Mild patches of water were found here and there. He noticed that he too was wearing clothes made of jasmine and twigs. There was a young girl shivering with fear and cold in the other end of the well. Her beauty fascinated Dominic. She had a child like face yet she had a buxom body. Her hands and legs looked long and delicate. Dominic looked at her with his kind eyes.

After a while, fruits and vegetables were thrown from above. Dominic shared it with the young girl who ate after a moment of hesitation. When time passed by, the girl got used to Dominic's presence and was curious to know more about him. She touched him. She discovered his shape and texture. She counted every inch of him, as a miser would do to his treasure. He discovered her body. He let his fingers experience the whole part by part. The touch communication turned them into a single beast with four legs, four hands, four eyes, two heads, two hearts, one heart and one soul. The soul battled within itself not wanting to spilt until sleep tamed it. They slept.

From the next day, the young girl began to teach him language, culture and religion.

'God created the world. He created animals. God wanted to create something that would give him eternal pleasure. He created women. The women roamed over the earth. God came down from heaven to make love to women. One day God realised that pleasure was short lived. He felt angry. Out of his anger the evil one was born. The evil one created men who chased God from the world. They began cheating women by pointing at stones and calling it God. The twin queens made the world a paradise by killing all men. They are the Gods now.' Terrible sounds were heard outside and soldiers thronged into the well using ropes made of creepers and pulled the young girl out. The young girl screamed and Dominic tried to protect her but was hit unconscious by one of the soldiers.

When Dominic woke up, he was tied to the roots of a banyan tree. Women came from nowhere and fed him with delicious sticky fruits. Dominic felt soulless. The two middle-aged queens took turns to make lust to him. Dominic screamed out of disgust.

It was night. A woman came close to him with food. He tried to kiss her with a sorrowful expression on his face. The woman looked around to see if anyone was watching them. The women untied him and escaped from there. He heard cries and screams but it was not her voice. He made fire to protect himself. He went into houses to find her but had to tame the women with his maleness when he could not find her.

Dominic entered a house of an old woman and saw her meditating among strange articles. The house was filled with smoke and he could not find anyone else in the house. When he was about to leave the old woman said 'You are from earth aren't you? I have your backpack. I have been collecting backpacks for years. I loved your Uncle. I do not know why he left me. I knew you would come. I will teach you everything. Our planet needs you. You have many women on your side. You can easily overthrow the greedy queens. You will be our king and the giver of children.'

'Where is the girl who I met in the well?' asked Dominic

'In prison for thinking there is life in another planet. The Queens think you are one of the survivors of the great disease'

In a few days, the woman called many angry women into her house and made everybody swear by the fire and attack the wicked Queens.

Dominic discovered his beloved once again. They shared their love with joy. As the promise he had given to the old women he used to make love with other women after his beloved got pregnant so that Zod would be saved. The soul of Zod was his soul. The sexual heat of Zod will always protect the king.

Dominic stopped masturbating. He felt as if he was reborn. He smiled at himself. He had brought his dead uncle to life and created a planet called Zod just to get into a suitable mood for masturbation. According to Dominic, masturbation is the ahimsa Satyagraha of the sexually starved masses. It united his senses into a constant feeling that was sublime. It was also a way through which he controlled his senses and hid his hard feelings. Masturbation took Dominic to another world where women did not care about their careers and wait until thirty to get married. Dominic remembered Shabri saying 'By the time you get to marry a woman you will be a middle aged philosopher with a middle aged wife if you take the sex only after marriage philosophy seriously. Our lawmakers and society sucks. They make us watch sexy shows on TV but do not give us a chance to get sexy. I want to be born in the Kamasutra era.'

'The Kamasutra era? When a few kings enjoyed women and money that were not theirs' and enslaved half of humankind,' Dominic had then replied.

'Have you heard about the Vedic period when women were treated as equals with men? That was centuries before the so-called Kamasutra era.' He added.

7

Fr. Ben entered the class to teach a paper called 'Communicative English'. He started the class with a few jokes about the funny nature of the English language and went on to introduce a topic on non-verbal communication. He gave an interesting lecture on eye contact, gestures and postures. He noticed Shabri writing something else and darted a question at him—'Shabri, Can you give an example for non-verbal communication?'

'Sex.' replied Shabri. There was a few seconds of silence. 'Sir!' Shabri continued, 'Doesn't it create a bond between humans which a thousand words cannot express? Regardless of religion, language, race, caste, creed, gender or species all beings communicate their deepest feelings in the language of sex. In sex, we are all one.'

Justine seemed to express a cultural shock. Sr. Monica coughed. Some students giggled; others sat making serious faces. All expected Fr. Ben to throw him out of the class.

'Smart!' said Fr. Ben, 'I never thought of it before. This is what they call thinking out of the box. Give a clap for your friend.'

A few students clapped. Dominic did not clap; he was lost in thoughts and scruples. Fr. Ben then went on to talk more on gestures that can leak your hidden emotions and the class went on as planned.

8

Man is a social animal.

Man is a political animal.

Man is a brainy animal.

Man is a selfish animal.

Man is a greedy animal.

Man is an irrational animal.

Man is a sexual animal.

Man is a heartless animal.

Man is an animal.

Women please take notes. (Written in my personal diary)

—Dominic Rodrigues

30.01.2010

9

I am Dominic Rodrigues. A novelist somewhere is trying to destroy my image before the reading public. I have wasted a lot of time trying to find him. He tries to communicate with me using strange ways I do not wish to describe. He even suggests where I should drop my reply. I have started suspecting my close friends. His identity remains a mystery to me. Beware of him! You may meet a person with kind eyes and will tell about your suffering to him; he will make you the morally deprived psychotic hero of his novel. I am here to tell my true story, which is very much different from the masala added melodramatic version of my story told by the novelist. Here is the truth—

I was born on 30.01.1988. My Gandhian Grandfather was very happy. I was the first son in the family after thirty years of hope (My mother's father had three daughters and my father's father had one son followed by four daughters). My Grandmother named me Dominic because she wanted me to become like St. Dominic Savio. She always wore frocks that were out fashioned in the1950's. I was breastfed for five years. Tribal women who lived in my neighbourhood who wore nothing to cover their breasts used to express their love by feeding me their milk without the knowledge of my family. My family learned about it quite late. I was taught to kiss the picture of Jesus Christ and say a few prayers that made no sense to me. 'Learning prayers are like putting money in the bank. It will benefit you when you grow old.' my grandmother said. 'Be obedient and don't lie. God and Jesus are watching you in their TV sets.' my mother said. 'Is Jesus watching you, Ma? How many TV sets does God have? How can God watch everybody?' I asked innocently. 'God only knows; it is sin to question God.' my mother replied. This question has always troubled me. My guess is that God is a huge being and all the stars are part of his body as cells are part of us. God is everything. He can feel when the tiniest part of his body hurts. It is not right to call God as 'He' because God has no penis. The black holes are God's vaginas;

God must be a woman. I had a fascination for the name 'Benizer Butto' that often came out the TV screens. My first fear came from viewing a giant animated mango that had a face of its own from the mango fruity advertisement. Once I saw a man dying on TV and asked my dad why people die, to which my dad replied, 'People die when their heart stops beating.' I held my little hands to my heart and wondered when it will stop beating; it was beating very fast. Whenever a character in the TV drove a car or a bike I would run into the kitchen and hide behind my mother's skirts hoping not to see a bloody accident. I was afraid of the famous giant sculpture of a Yakshi (Female spirit/demoness) I saw in a garden near Malampurzha Dam. I feared the skull I saw in my backyard the same way I feared the skeleton I saw in a museum. My father made feel the skull and bones inside my flesh and skin. 'What you fear is inside you.' he said. I learnt to read from the Women's Era magazine, which systematically came to my house. I poured fish curry over a Brahmin girl's head and created a riot in my play school. I stepped in the shoes of John the Baptist when I should have been St. Dominic Savio. I always wanted my father to carry me. My father told me that he is importing a robot from the United States, which is designed to carry children so high that they would cry when they reach near the skies. After that, no child will want to be carried. However, my father carried me to the operation theatre to repair a hole in my heart. Even to this day I can feel the vacuum created by the hole in my heart were all my flawed emotions are hiding. On returning from the hospital in a train, police asked us to put down the shutters. People were throwing stones at the train because they thought that we killed Rajiv Gandhi. The train did not move. The driver's head was bleeding. We were escorted by the police to Palakkad— to the coconut trees, to the rice bowl of Kerala, to the place were once remained a beautiful forest. I always liked to take long walks from my house away from the housing colony. As the road gets narrow, the houses become huts and the sounds of brawling hens become louder. I would end my walk when I reach the green paddy fields, which touched the horizon. I would sit on a milestone with my eyes closed and enjoy the breeze from the paddy fields. I would collect strange leaves, flowers and nests. I would get beats and scolding from my grandparents for coming late. There were many snakes in the paddy fields. The newspaper carried news about the death of young children due to snakebites. Today young children die due to road accidents: modernisation! Once I saw a viper in the bathroom when I went to pee. My father killed it. It gave me the creeps. When I went walking in the evening rat snakes used to swiftly cross the road before me. My heart used to stop for a moment. My friends believed that snakes were Gods and one should not kill them if one is not so found of death curses. There was a man in our neighbourhood who was called the Snake-man from the age of twelve because he was found of trapping snakes. He was such a brave man. He once conducted a street show in which he put a king cobra around his neck while his wife had a python around her hips. He looked like the incarnation of God Shiva. He died of snakebite when he accidently kicked a camouflaged snake while he was drawing water from the well. 'The snake-curse: it killed him.' my friends used to say. I always liked to ask questions. Sometimes my neighbours got so irritated that they replied 'Because the sky is so high and you are so very low' as the answer. Being an Anglo-Indian I knew to speak English better than anyone at school. Some were surprised at my fluency. Others mocked at me telling me that I am an Englishman coming to take their freedom away. One part of me wanted to run away and be settled in Australia or USA and another part of me wanted to go to the Himalaya seeking eternal spiritual bliss. In both the cases, the inspiration came from the movies. I was a big fan of Australian cricketer Ricky Ponding and cheered for him when he played against India. I hated the noisy Anglo-Indian parties with old wine, old songs and old women. Probably I was too young to enjoy them. I had a few friends. I was lonely most of the times. It is the same loneliness, which followed me like a shadow for the rest of my life. [To be continued]

10

Dominic was very unhappy in Assisi College because he felt that the college management was dominating over the students. Cameras were put all over the campus to monitor the movements of the students everywhere except in the administrative block where the principal and other administrative officers had their rooms. Mobile phones were totally banned. If they were found, they will be confiscated. 'Mobile phones have become like a part of the body these days. My Mobile is my soul, my identity and my parallel self. The people who run this college are born castrators.' said Shabri. The teachers always warned the students of the chances of them being expelled or being made to pay huge fines. Dominic watched many students being brutally scolded with filthy words by the Vice-Principal for silly reasons while he waited without patience for a signature in his train ticket concession form.

Dominic had come from a very peaceful environment. Unlike the hot climate of Chennai, his village had rains all the time. No education institute he went treated children like this. His school was known for its democratic values. His previous college gave a lot of importance to the development of freedom among students. In Assisi, it was the first time he was being taught by male teachers. All his previous educational experiences were filled with the love and support of kindhearted women unlike his mother's experience in a convent run by nuns who were known for their heartlessness. A nun once made every child drink a small spoon of orange juice mixed with urine when no one was ready to reveal to the nuns anything about the identity of the beautiful young girl who urinated in the orange juice mend for the nuns. Dominic's mother said 'Nuns, who had complexes because they could not have children, physically and mentally abused little children without any reason.' Dominic remembered the stories his mother told him when he came to Assisi. Instead of the nuns, the priests made life as good as hell. Of course, a few like Fr.Ben used to be very liberal with students.

After his first year in class he wrote on the board 'Arse see see' and made his classmates laugh. Luckily, the camera did not see this.

Dominic was more unhappy in the hostel were there were more rules to torture the students. All students were made to remain silent once they entered the Hostel at seven. No one was allowed to leave his rooms. Even for going to toilet, they had to get special permissions during this time. Every student experienced a solitary confinement during this period. Many students were sent out of the hostel and college for simple reasons. Students were blackmailed into studies since anyone who got low grades were sent out immediately.

Dominic often compared the priests to the Pharisees and Sadducees of the Bible who follow rules unaware of higher Christian values like love and forgiveness. Some thing, which made Dominic happy, was the friends he won in Assisi. Though he was an introvert, his friends encouraged him to be more social.

11

Once, Dominic decided to go to the Hostel mess through a newly found short cut. The warden called him and asked him why he did not come through the normal road. Dominic narrated a few lines from the poem 'The Road Not Taken'. 'The road not taken leads to hell', said the warden and locked him in the generator room without letting him eat his dinner for the rest of the night and promised him that he would be dismissed if he does not come through the normal road.

When Dominic narrated this incident to Shabri, he said 'If you be a normal kid you will be punished for a sin you never knew. If you commit a crime after a good plan and preparation no one will punish you.'

Justine on the other hand warned Dominic about breaking the rules.

12

Dominic hated the system, the rules and the administrators so much that he would often think of ways to destroy them. He would spend hours thinking of the stories about the vile priests dominates over the students. This made him depressed.

If one had a chance to look at Dominic's face at that moment one would not see any emotion in his eyes. His lips would be tightly shut. One cannot see the illogical poking heat flowing inside his brain cells.

13

Assisi College invited famous writer Jagan Raj to inaugurate an English workshop. Dominic sat silently and watched. 'Any questions?' asked the MC. A girl doing her under graduation in visual communication and journalism got up and asked a question. Dominic did not understand the question but was mystified by her delicate movements. Dominic could not understand why she looked so beautiful. His heart began to knock violently from inside. It must be wanting to come out and join other hearts, especially the hearts of beautiful women like the girl who asked the question.

14

Marga, a Tibetan restaurant, was located a kilometre away from Assisi. All the repressed emotions between the girls and boys of Assisi was said to be resolved here. Four red-filmed CFL bulbs lit the entire restaurant. The small TV never changed its obsession from Channel V. The free sauce was said to have the taste of romance.

When Dominic was eating Momoos in the restaurant the girl who asked the question was sitting next to him. 'Hi' she said taping the hands of a boy who sat next to her. Dominic smelled her perfume. Dominic smelled something else.

15

A theatre company visited the college to select students for their next production 'The Modern Macbeth Machine'. Only Dominic was selected from Assisi College. Dominic saw the girl who asked the question standing near him.

'Did you come for the auditions?' asked Dominic

'No, I am planning to write a report about the play in the newspaper. I am doing Journalism. So you are Dominic.'

'Yes, and you are?'

'Manju'

'Sweet name'

'Thank you. Why did you take MA English Literature? Is it because you love drama?'

'I love books. I also want to become a screenwriter. What do you want to be?'

'What do you think I am studying journalism for?'

16

Manju said to Dominic 'The short story you wrote was very good. It makes one fall in love with you.'

'Really!'

'I loved the way you made the woman the central attraction though she said only one sentence in a male dominated story. You also have a naughty little brain'

'It is not that little as you imagine. My story is neither male dominated nor female dominated.'

'Love makes you discover who you really are.' thought Dominic.

17

Dominic took out his mobile phone, which had gone into hiding because of the rules, and send Manju a text message:

When I look into your eyes I see the black moon I see the black sea I see the divine pearl I see nothingness the picture of my heart my soul

The second text message:

Your eyes are like the black grape the divine gem floating over the milk of the universe.

In the beginning, Manju did not reply. When she began to reply, she sent weird messages that could baffle any mad lover.

'Love is a return into the joys of childhood.' thought Dominic.

18

When the college ended, Dominic used to wait at Marga for Manju and had a long conversation. One day Manju said 'I am leaving college early tomorrow. I am so exited. I am going to meet my boyfriend. He came from Hyderabad just to see me.'

'It is better to have loved and lost . . .' thought Dominic; but his hopes were still intact. He wanted the boyfriend to be just a male friend. He wanted them to argue and break up. He wanted the boyfriend to die because of a crime he had committed in his previous birth.

19

'Your short film got selected to be screened on a TV reality show! You should give me a party.' said Dominic. Dominic and Manju were doing some official work all alone in the principal's office. Manju showed Dominic a few videos on an African dance in her laptop.

'Aren't they good?' asked Manju

'Pretty'

'Shall we dance and continue the thousand year old ritual?'

'But this is the principal's office'

'No cameras in the principal's office remember'

Dominic and Manju danced. Dominic felt a kind of joy he had not felt before. Even though they danced only for half an hour these golden moments echoed inside Dominic's heart for days. He could feel the warmth of her hands in his. Dominic decided that he was surely in love. The memory of a possible boyfriend faded away.

20

When Dominic attained the knowledge of his previous births, he was busy thinking about of his exams and leaving Assisi as soon as possible. He was filled with a kind of wisdom that brought peace to his mind. He had attained the eternal peace. He will never go unhappy again. Dominic looked at the notice board that announced about the inter-departmental singing and dance completions that will start in a few hours. His friends had forced him to enrol against his wishes.

Dominic always shied away from such competitions because he had to mingle with people. He secretly loved singing and dancing but he always choose to be lonely. His participation in plays was his only romance with the outside world. 'Why am I always hiding myself? Is it laziness? Is it because the world ignores me?' he always wondered. He had spent two years in Assissi grumbling over the rules and circumstances.

'I will not cancel my registration.' thought Dominic with a smile and thought about the times he was called Padmini.

21

ACT ONE

Chorus:

Like the story of God and man,

Like the story of the lover and the beloved,

Like the story of the fox and the crow,

Is this dialogue—this drama—this waste of time.

[Enter Novelist with a book]

Novelist: It is easy to love a book. It is easy to hate one. I do not promise love or hate. I only promise an experience. I am here to ask questions and not to give answers. You will comprehend the problems of the world but not its solutions. You will see it all through the eyes of Dominic who is the protagonist but not the hero of this novel. He will prove to you how foolish he is; I am only an instrument or medium that trumpets his lack of sanity. I request you all not to follow his footsteps; you may become an egocentric scum just like him.

[Smoke hides the stage. Dominic appears. He is standing on the novelist's book]

Dominic: You have no right to tell my story to the world. Your ideas about me are false. Your story is wrong and meaningless. You are confusing people.

Novelist: Call me Sappho Dionysus! I am the omniscient narrator. I know everything. I will tell the TRUTH.

Dominic: You will not! You cannot! You do not know the truth.

22

Raguvaran and Laxmi prayed for years for a child. Padmini was born. The mother smelled the baby. It was the smell of innocence. The smell made her breasts fill with the milk of affection. Raruvaran took away the baby away and said, 'Remember the promise. She must not live like us; she is born for a divine duty.'

'But my breasts are full. I need to feed the child.'

Raguvaran sucked the milk from her breasts. She was not satisfied.

They sacrificed their daughter to the temple of God Purisha as the promise she had made. The temple priestess took the baby in her hands and said 'This girl will change the world'. She brought up Padmini as her own daughter. She watched the natural changes of Padmini's body as if it was a miracle. She taught her the various arts. She feared that Padmini would beat her in the arts for which she was famous.

When Padmini danced, the whole village was provoked to dance with her. Her hips moved rhythmically like a planet, which was seducing its two moons, her breasts. The vibrancy and vigour of her body silenced and nullified everything else that was around and made her look like the only entity that possessed life. Her movements were in tune with the rhythms of nature; it seemed to hypnotise nature itself. Her figure was divinity personified.

When Padmini sang the whole village sang with her. Sometimes they remained silent. It was the greatest moment in their lives. An orphan remembered the times when his mother smiled at him. A middle-age woman remembered the calm air and the flowers she saw before her marriage. An old man remembered the first time he had made love with a beautiful girl who died years ago. Her voice had something.

After she finished her song, the priestess hugged her. She felt the heat of her body. For a moment, she forgot that she was a teacher. She soon came back to her senses and looked at Padmini with a serious face.

The temple priestess said 'Every girl will meet her man—her god. She will overflow with joy of sacrificial love. She will dance only for him after that. She will sing only for him. He will give you the gift of sexual satisfaction that will lead you to God—the eternal creator.'

'What is sexual intercourse? Why do men tease girls in the name of sex?' asked the doubtful Padmini.

'Sex is that which created you. God might have created the sun, the stars and the universe. God might have created the brain, the mind and the soul. Still, sex is God's greatest creation. Sex connects anything to everything. Sex connects the body to the mind and the mind to the soul. Everything you see around you is the power of sex. You live for it; you die for it. You get children because of sex. You are born to have sex; you die because the sexual energy in you is lost. You eat to get energy to have sex. You earn money and do other works to buy sex through marriage. You have talents and skills so that you can make sex better. You sleep to refresh your sexual energy. Every time you breathe, you steal some sexual energy that is hidden in the air. We can't see God but we can feel and experience him when we have sex. Virginity is death and sex is life. Padmini, my girl, you have a very flexible body. I think you will enjoy the divine sex and attain nirvana, the divine salvation, before anyone of your age can.'

Padmini was confused.

23

Padmini heard from an old man at the temple, 'The whole world is Maya. An illusion created by God. Our flesh is just biotic matter and bones hard stone. The only reality is the soul. As gopis wish to merge with Krishna, all souls wish to merge with the supreme soul. Love and worship are the ways to reach God.'

'Love and worship is not sex. These are the greater things which humans can't understand fully.' thought Padmini.

The temple priestess said 'When you bathe you should feel the cold water making love to you. When you cloth yourself feel the warmth with which your clothes cuddle you with. When you touch the mud, feel its softness seducing you. When you hold a stone, feel its hardness conquering you. When it rains, feel every drop kissing you and touching you kindly and rudely. Feel the wind pushing you away and pulling you close like a naughty lover. When you eat, feel the food kissing your lips and entering into you like a passionate lover. Every object has a soul. Every moment in your life is a moment close to the eternal sexual wisdom. Sexual acts help you to elevate your soul so that it can merge with God.'

Padmini started believing in everything that the priestess said. She was fascinated about sex like the other girls who played with her.

24

When Padmini was fourteen, she was sent to a school. Both male and female teachers demonstrated different sexual positions as the boys and girls watched. They made acrobatic movements with miraculous flexibility. Legs and hands moved in such a way that it was difficult to guess, at first sight, whether a leg or a hand belonged to a man or a woman. The ferocity of the males frightened the students. They choreographed multiple movements and postures with ease; the women were mere puppets who were dancing to their tunes. The men pulled the women up and made them swing in the air; they caught hold of their legs, held the women upside down and nibbled on their secret places. The women tried their best to support themselves by standing on their legs or hands. The men twisted them forward, backward and sideward and savoured the parts they found to be delicious. Whenever the women made a move, they overpowered them by tickling their delicate parts and softly biting them on their lips, breasts and belly. All the ornaments that the women wore were used as chains to control their movements. They devoured every breath, sigh or voice that came from the women. The male teachers took the lead and it looked like they were going to win the battle of love, but then the women with their delicate hands easily disarmed the strong muscles of men and with their soft lips and tongues managed to make the men flow. The men lay down exhausted and the women fanned them to sleep singing lullabies. Padmini wondered if this was the reality. 'Was all of this made up?' she asked herself. The students were then given live non-poisonous snakes to play with. They felt the vigour of the snakes in their hands. At night, the girls were made to touch each other and feel the sexual energy flowing through their bodies. The girl who felt Padmini was filled with a special kind of energy that she felt waves of divine fire flowing through her veins. She loved Padmini and knew she was special even though she could not express her love for Padmini. Stories about love and lust were narrated. One of the stories, which made Padmini think, was the story of sage Jhothi.

"Jhothi was a young girl who left home in order to become a sage. She had made a promise that she will never marry anyone born on this earth as a human male. She meditated for years following the strict rules of chastity. She gave all the food she had to a stray dog that followed her wagging its tail. She learned all the Vedas and holy texts. She knew she was near to eternal salvation. All of a sudden, she remembered the story of sage Mandapala. Sage Mandapala had heard many stories about men and women who ruined their lives because of their extreme lusts and just like Jhothi decided not to feel lust. He wanted to reach the divine one. 'It is our sexual desires which keeps us away from the divine one.' he thought. He left human settlements and went to live in the forest. He practiced yoga and controlled all his desires. He learned all the divine secrets and achieved the impossible. Like every other human being he died. He reached the gates of heaven.

The gatekeeper asked, 'Have you made another human being feel love?'

Mandapala was silent.

'Have you enjoyed the moment of joy when you gave birth to a baby?'

Silence again.

'Tell me about the warmth of the kiss of a young woman? Why are you silent? Go back to earth as a female bird and sacrifice your life for your children forgetting about your husband who you love so much and the heavens will be yours.'

Mandapala did as the gatekeeper said.

Sage Jhothi realised the seriousness of the promise she had made. Using her divine powers, she turned the stray dog that was sitting beside her into a human male. She made love with the male and later gave birth to a baby girl. The human male wanted spend more time in lust whereas sage Jhothi wanted to spent more time in meditation. The human male started to become more and more aggressive. Sage Jhothi turned him back into a dog. Sage Jhothi like any other mother taught her daughter about the secrets of the world before she became one with God. Every time the daughter was in trouble, a dog would come from nowhere to rescue her. The dog became woman's best friend."

25

Padmini wrote a poem:

I wait in the darkness.

I wait at daylight.

My patience is losing its endurance.

Will you just come, O Lord?

In my dream, I felt your breath,

Your smell, your taste, your touch,

Your voice, your sight, your might . . .

Why did you end my dream?

I bathed, I ate, I dressed

I danced, I sang, I jumped

I was a good girl all the time

But you did not come

Break the shield of my lips with your tongue.

Break the shield of my heart with your voice.

Break the shield of my womb with your arrow.

Break the virginity of my eyes with your sighs.

I will give you everything.

My body, my mind, my soul.

Will you burn me

With the fire of my own love?

Renounce your bodily fluids

Into my treasure chest

And I will turn the seed into trees

Which will walk into the shadows of future.

I want to die—

When I lose my sexual energy.

When your kisses smother me.

When your soul steals me away.

I will be reborn in love.

If love is just a touch

I do not ask so much

I just want to be your dove.

26

The wise young man entered. All raised with respect. He came close to Padmini's ears and said 'You would not find God. God will find you. He will make you His lover. He will steal your soul and make it His. Imagine you have billions of vaginas and imagine that all your vaginas experience the divine orgasm that no woman has ever experienced. That be the pleasure you feel when you meet God.'

Padmini looked at him and admired his masculine beauty.

He went on to the next girl and whispered something into her ears. He never spoke anything so that everyone would hear. His messages were personal messages.

The wise young man was chased from the temple for some reason.

27

It was Padmini's wedding night. She was exited to the fact that she was going to meet her god. She was naked. Her hair was so long that it tickled her bottom. She wore a lily on her hair. She had sandalwood rubbed all over her body. She sat on a white mat made of jasmine. There were oil lamps and rose petals all around her. There was light everywhere. The holiness of the lamps reflected on her glowing golden brown skin making it prettier. Her breasts and hips were so curvaceous that it made her look like a divine idol. She imagined how her husband would look like. She imagined a man hugging her and taking care of her. The man of her imagination resembled her father who she had never seen.

She heard her husband making his entry. She smiled without looking at his face. She wanted him to pour water over her, wash the sandalwood paste, say sweet words in her ears, touch her softly, discover her and make love to her.

He kicked the oil lamps. The hot oil burned Padmini's skin.

'You should have moved.' said the husband, 'why did you not wash off your sandalwood shit off your impure body? You look like a dirty pig.'

Padmini took the clay pot and poured all the water over her.

'Why did you not keep any water for me?' asked the loving husband.

'Because . . .'

'Shut up!! Good girls do not speak. They just do. If you are a good wife you will first think about your husband and then think your personal needs.'

The husband whipped the wife. The husband pinched the wife. It gave him immense pleasure. He laughed alone.

The husband made lust to the wife.

The wife could not feel the love.

Love is not that touch.

28

The husband asked his friend 'Will you give me those gold statues if I let you sleep with my wife?'

'Provided she sings her famous song "I wait in the darkness" while I make love to her.'

29

Padmini cried after the fifth man crushed her under him. Each man had stabbed her natural wound as many times possible. She felt as if she is being cut into pieces. The image that ran inside her mind was that of ugly dry skinned snakes. The snakes were around her neck chocking her to death. Men are like ghosts who take your soul away and leave you to die.

'You bitch! You whore! Who told you to sleep with other men?' said the husband in public. The whip licked Padmini's blood.

30

Padmini wrote a poem:

I know what love is:

It is

Just a trap for your soul;

Just a torturing machine;

Just a laugh at pains;

Just a lustful touch;

Just a sharp sword that enters inside your most painful wound.

31

After sleeping with the temple priestess, Padmini's husband asked for another girl he could use to make money.

'I will help you get married to any of the girls I have but they would not be as beautiful as Padmini.' replied the priestess.

32

Padmini smiled at a man she hated. 'Open the doors of your house at mid-night and I will teach you what real love is,' said the man. At midnight, Padmini whispered into the man's ear 'How soft is my skin?'

'It is softer than the feathers of the Okia bird.'

'Poke your knife into my husband's throat and I will be your slave forever. Tie me to a tree and torture my body with yours for hours and I will not scream. Rub sticky jaggery on my breasts and bite them and I will not scream'.

The man's knife was polluted with blood. He turned around and saw a naked woman riding his horse. The naked woman realised the similarities of shape between the hair on the horse's mane and her pubic hair as she travelled on.

A middle-aged man who saw the woman on the horse from a distance repented and asked forgiveness to the goddess whom he rebuked. He built a temple on that very spot.

A thief who was known for womanising found a horse with a naked woman sleeping on it by the banks of a lonely river. The thief brought the horse and the woman to his house. He raped a silent Padmini. 'I better not let her die.' he thought. He fed her fruits dipped in honey. Padmini became healthier. The thief recited a poem to seduce Padmini:

"The female organ is like the head of a lion.

The male organ is like the head of an elephant.

The elephant willingly put his trunk

Into the mouth of the lion.

Though the elephant looks big

The lion is the king of the jungle."

After playing as the king of the jungle, Padmini fed him with some poison; she had seen the destructive lust in his eyes.

She continued her journey. At nights, she lay on the streets. Merchants raped her, soldiers raped her; old men raped her, young men raped her. When beggars raped her she smiled and thought, 'this is what they call love.' She realised that she did not have the gift to give birth.

Padmini decided to die. 'I will ride my horse into the desert and starve to death there. The person who finds my dead body will find it skinny and ugly and would not feel like raping it.'

She starved in the deserts. She left her horse to its destiny. She took a bunch of hot sand and put it over her head and prayed, 'God forgive me for I have killed many. I found no other way. I do not know what to do and what not to do. I do not know what is right and what is wrong. From henceforth I will not judge anyone. I will not kill anyone. I will not treat anyone as my enemy. Forgive me and let me live.'

A young man found her unconscious and took her to his hut. He gave her some dates and water. Padmini found the wise man who once whispered in her ears smiling at her.

'So you are the man of wisdom. With wisdom or not all men are cruel beings who love to torture women', said Padmini.

'Your experiences may say so. But the truth is far away.' said the young man.

'What is truth?'

'Truth is destiny. It is away from man but it resides in him. It is away from pleasure but is in joy. It is away from rituals but is in a prayerful heart. It is away from the attractive but is in beauty. It is away from fondness but is in love. You who lived in the land of illusions have not felt it. The people who brought you up believed in illusions and not in the divine arts that leads towards the truth. I was cursed by your people when I talked to them about their mistakes.'

'What are the divine arts? Can you teach them to me?'

'They are the arts of the body, the arts of the mind and the arts of the soul. Since you lived in a culture, which has ignored the arts of the mind and the soul, I shall not teach them to you. You must remember that the arts of the body include the arts of pleasure, health and defence. Your society taught you only the art of pleasure without knowing its true meaning. Your society is still in pain. Sexuality is a great truth but it is also a grand illusion that can serve the evils of greed and lust. Sex, passion, religion, friendship, prayer, rituals, honesty, faithfulness, beauty, charity, kindness and forgiveness are only roads leading to the Love, the ultimate Truth. Every being is blessed with the divine sexual energy. This sexual energy should not be used as an instrument of lust neither should it be repressed into the depths of the mind; it should be sublimated into great actions. Great actions include glorifying your body through dance, music and meditation and giving yourself in service to humanity. Your sexual energy can be used to comfort the orphaned, the poor and the unloved. It can be used to give hope to the aged through small kind deeds. It can be used to show care, empathy, compassion and gentleness to all beings on earth. You should love everyone but sexual bonding should happen only with one special person who loves and respects you. When the male organ goes inside it says to the female soul, "I am offering all my love, care, body, blood, mind and soul to you because I love and respect your divine force and would be content with it for eternity. I worship the God in your body, mind and soul; I worship the God in my body, mind and soul." The female matrix says the male soul, "I accept your offering with the same love, kindness and respect you have for me. I give and receive the divine force that makes the universe alive. My love and your love is one; my soul and your soul is one. I worship the God in your body, mind and soul; I worship the God in my body, mind and soul." Such is the greatness of lovemaking. In sight, it may look physical but it begins a spiritual thread that goes on and on for thousands of years flying as a man made kite that represents the halo of humanity.'

The wise young man taught Padmini the arts of health and defence. He treated her as his daughter.

'Are you my God?' she asked.

'No.' said the wise man and pointed his finger towards a distant village.

33

On the way, she met the priestess who had taught her. She pulled her hands and said, 'Come back you evil one.'

'You were the one who left me in the hands of the evil one.' Padmini pushed her to the ground. The priestess changed into the wise young man. 'I was only testing you. Come, let's copulate.'

'No,' said Padmini, 'You are not him.' The wise young man changed into Padmini's husband. 'I am a changed man. A sage saved my life and taught me the arts of the mind and the soul. Forgive me and come with me and I will teach you everything I know. I will not hurt you again.'

'I forgive you,' said Padmini, 'but I have my own path to travel. You who have understood the great arts will surely understand me.'

The figure of her husband transformed into a dove and disappeared.

Something made her lose all her hope once again. She had the feeling that no one really cares about her. She will never learn all the divine arts. The whole of humankind is only trying to befool her with their philosophies. When she reached a stream, she looked into it and said to herself, 'I am the ugliest person on earth. Everything I see and experience is just maya, an illusion, the rays of a dead star, the smoke from a burned universe.'

34

When Padmini woke up one morning, she found herself naked with mud and slime sticking to her skin. She walked into a jungle. She washed herself in a stream. She found a white sari flowing with the current. She wore it and continued her journey. She reached a small village. People started noticing her.

'So these are the people who are going to rape me tonight' she thought. She entered the temple gate. The people were astonished. A wind blew. All the bells tolled. The door to the idol opened. It was going to rain. Padmini looked into the eyes of goddess Yoni. 'Gods are just stones' she thought. She suddenly knew why people were looking at her. No woman was allowed to enter the temple of goddess Yoni. She was looking at something no woman had seen before—the curvaceous nude statue of Goddess Yoni standing in her famous slanting posture.

Padmini imitated the posture of the Goddess with a sarcastic smile on her face. 'Today is my last day on earth. These men are going to behead me for my crime. Hope they rape me, cut me into pieces and hang it in the streets as a warning before they experience their true love.' She thought.

When Padmini looked back all the villagers were bowing before her and shouted.

'Devi! Bless us!'

'Hail! Virgin of virgins!'

'Hail! Queen of heaven!'

'Hail! Mother of purity!'

'Hail! Symbol of chastity!'

'Hail! Creator, protector and destroyer!'

'All powerful! All Powerful! All powerful!'

They cried with joy and praised.

Padmini took courage and spoke in an authoritative voice 'I am Goddess Yoni.' There was sound of thunder, which reduced everyone except Padmini to shivers. It rained.

An old priest took courage and said 'Ohm! Hail Devi! We knew about you arrival. Only the Goddess will be brave enough to enter a temple were women are forbidden. The bells tolled and the sacred door opened to signal your divine arrival. Rain has fallen after so many months because of your blessing. This is no rain but holy water.'

Another elder priest said 'Show mercy on us!! We all respect your divine presence. I knew you are our Devi before anyone could. Is not this white sari the one which the Gods presented to you when you slew the demon Kalasura?'

'Yes.' said Padmini with a new dignity 'I bless you all. I have decided to reside in this temple for the next hundred years unless my soul escapes from me to participate in the glorious heavenly duties. You will have to serve me. I will solve all your problems.'

34

Padmini preached 'I looked into the earth. It was filled with sin. My anger knew no bounds. I wanted to destroy the earth but the Gods pleaded with me. Therefore, I decided to take a human form and reside in your village that is the centre of the world—henceforth I rename this village as Padmini. The old name should not be uttered again. I made a figure out of clay and sandalwood and poured life into it. I allowed the body to roam on earth. When the right time came, I entered into the body and came to your village. The body that I am in may not last forever but I will. From henceforth, women shall enter the temple. They should sing and dance to please me. I will teach them the arts of the body and they will teach it to you. You men should take care of household activities when the women are worshiping me. In return, I shall teach you to make love in a divine manner, which will give you greater pleasure. You shall not steal or rape. You should help the poor and needy. Remember you share your soul with them. No one should go hungry. You should make yourself strong and be my divine army. You should love everyone and make each other happy. Then you will find yourself happy. Look at the image in your fellow being's eye. It is your image, it is his or her image and it is the image of God. That is when you realize who you are. You will be declared wise by the Gods and will be united with the heavens once you die.'

All the villagers were surprised at her wisdom.

'Divine words are so wise that they shatter all human voices away. Hail to thee! Devi!' cried the high priest.

Padmini talked to the village women and found out that their lives and philosopies were very different from what she had learned from the priestess. Even though the women did not enjoy religious or political powers they were happy to live with their families. The men were faithful to them and helped them with their daily work with care and understanding. 'The greatest joy comes when you work in the fields with your husband beside you and you know that you are the reason for the order in the society; you know that you are the real master who controls the feelings in the minds of men.' said one of the village women.

35

The village of Padmini was reborn with a new zest. All people were happy. They felt that their lives have been changed. They rose up in pride when they knew that other villagers envied them. As Goddess Yoni commanded them, they kept the Goddess' presence in the village as a secret to the rest of the world.

Padmini stayed in the underground chamber of the temple. She lit all the oil lamps in the chamber to discover its beauty. There was a small pond in the middle with cold water. The water came from a tunnel, which was from the direction of the forest. The walls were full of moss. Wild creepers, which bore blue flowers, created tiny cracks on the pillars. Padmini liked the solitude she enjoyed in the chamber. She did not let anyone to enter her chamber.

36

One night when Padmini was eating the offerings of her devotees, she heard a few footsteps in her room. She thought of screaming but that would be unwise. A young naked man entered and walked towards the fireplace and watched the fire eating up the woods. He had come through the tunnel. He cried silently. He was tall and handsome. He was not brave enough to look at her eyes. He left after an hour.

The man showed himself at the same time for a whole week. Padmini patiently watched him.

37

In Padmini's dream, the wise man appeared and said 'You have found your God. He will be your husband forever. You will discover the truth that you are God. What you said before the people is true. Billions of years back God felt very lonely. The angels whom He created could not give Him company. Angels were just shadows and echoes of His own soul. He thought of creating His masterpiece—Homo sapiens. He divided Himself into two parts—power and beauty. His power He called man and His beauty He called woman. The woman stormed into earth—rivers started to flow and trees started to grow. The man stormed into the world—wars began, palaces built, countries made and civilization cherished. You need to control the man to control earth. Padmini, go into him, unite yourself with your other self and become God, go into him, Padmini, go into him. The man who entered your chamber is God who is yet to discover himself. He has lost his power. Help him discover it.'

So saying the wise man touched Padmini's cheeks. Padmini could feel the touch even after she woke up.

38

The young man entered Padmini's chamber as usual. She was not wearing any clothes. She wearing ornaments made of jasmine flowers around her arms and thighs. A thin golden chain, which was presented to her by the villagers, lay around her neck. A black thread that was presented to her by the priestess before her marriage lay around her waist. A disobedient branch of the thick thread tickled her genitals. The priestess believed that the thread had magical properties that could help in the seduction of a man. She wore the silver anklets that she found from a rotten corpse in the desert.

'Where is your sari?' asked the man.

'It is drying.'

'I live in the forest. My mother died few months ago. I buried her and threw her sari into the stream. I found you wearing it.'

'Do you want it back?'

'No, my mother told that the person who finds her sari will save me.'

'Who are you, young man?'

'I am God. That is what my mother called me.'

'I know. I am also a God.'

Padmini narrated her story to God.

God patiently listened and left when Padmini finished her story.

39

The next day Padmini put some food into God's mouth. She felt his mouth that was warm. His teeth looked perfect for a man who lived in the forest. He thanked her. Padmini brushed his hair with her fingers. They were soft. She smelled his hair. The fresh water of the stream, were Padmini found the sari, echoed in the smell. She kissed his eyes. She gently bit his lower lip and tasted it with her tongue. She sucked his chin and felt its strength. She touched his shoulders and felt his hard flesh and bones. She did never have a chance to appreciate male beauty before. All her experiences were violent passions. She kissed his chest. She got the smell of male sweat; she tasted it. She touched his hard stomach and felt his muscles bubbling within as he breathed; she breathed over it. The breath of her mouth made it harder.

'Want to hear a song?' she asked him.

Padmini hugged him and sang a tune in his ears. Padmini put all her passions into the silent song. He could feel the heat of Padmini's breath falling on his cheeks. He could also feel the heat of Padmini's femininity rousing on his thighs. She tasted him again. Her various taste buds were roused. It was sweet and salty. It was succulent. The softness of her tongue made his masculinity shiver and sigh. Her lips, which were large and thick, could powerfully control his hardness. With her tiny hands, she held his strong thighs that stood like unmovable roots. He felt as if he was melting into her. A spark was lit in God's mind—a revelation, 'this is how a mother will feel when she breastfeeds her baby with the milk of affection.' God said it to Padmini. She felt something in her bosom.

Padmini rubbed oil on his body and gave him a bath in cold water. When he shivered, Padmini hugged him again. God felt her warm soft flesh. He gently pushed her away from him. Padmini smiled and began to dance. Her hips moved gracefully. There was a sparkle in her large eyes, which were trying to grasp God's expressions. God looked at her with admiration. Padmini felt as if she was the most beautiful woman on earth.

God left before dawn.

40

'I have realised that you are a part of me and I am a part of you' said God to Padmini. 'I love you more than I love myself'

Padmini smiled.

They sat opposite to each other and felt the shapes of each other's bodies. The beauty of every curve, line and mark was magnified by these touches. They touched each other's genitals. God said 'We are different yet we are the same.'

Padmini replied 'You don't understand. Your genitals are mine and my genitals are yours. Our genitals are one. It is actually the connection between us just like the mother to the child, by the umbilical cord. They are made for each other. Together they form the universe. Every living creature is born from its divinity.'

Padmini picked up a feather of a crow, which was a present from god, and tickled God's body with it. She moved the feather slowly over his body like a sculptor who removes the tiny dust particles in order to enjoy the true beauty of his masterpiece. God picked up the most beautiful rose from the offerings and feathered Padmini's body with it. The colour of the rose seemed to enter into her skin.

After their tongue and the breaths felt every inch of their bodies, they interlocked their lips to discover another connection between them.

Padmini squeezed the juice of a mango on her breasts. God tasted the juice with hunger and said 'I worship you'. The heat of his breath stabbed her chest. 'I worship you, too' she replied. 'We must prepare ourselves to become one' said Padmini. They rubbed oil over each other and bathed in the temple pond. They used mud to purify themselves. God made sure that every bit of Padmini's body was clean and pure; Padmini made sure that every bit of God's body was clean and pure.

They looked at each other's eyes. They cheered with joy. Their wet bodies wetted each other. They lay on the bed and wrestled to overpower each other with love. Padmini's vagina was like an infant mouth that sucks the milk of love into it. She accepted God's milk offering with bliss. They sacrificed their bodies to each other and danced to the tunes of instinct. They repeated the oldest divine ritual of creation that would not lose its continuity for billions of years; the ritual discovered nature in its wildest form. The moment lasted for eternity. Padmini cried out of pleasure. Padmini felt as if she was making love to God in mid space as all the stars and planets merged into them to become one. Padmini felt as if she had billions of vaginas that were roused into infinite orgasmic pleasures by the power of the divine energy. She remembered what the wise man said. 'I love you. I love you' she said repeatedly.

'I love you, too.' said God and started dancing to a faster tune.

After making love, Padmini put her ears over God's chest and listened to the rhythm of his heart.

'I can feel the whole universe that is dancing to the beats of your heart.' she said. God took her hand and listened to her pulse. 'I can feel the same. You are God. I felt if before you told me. I feel like God when I make love to you. The God in you has flowed into me. My mother was right. Before meeting you, I was a lonely forest man but now I am God. My mother named me rightly. You are the mother of mothers.'

God left when Padmini fell asleep. No one knew what happened.

41

The next day when Padmini met crowds of people a man asked her, 'How many times should one make love to be really satisfied in life?'

'Just once', replied Padmini to the shock of all the men present there. 'Men may have sex many times out of lust but they would not be satisfied. Mere action does give pleasure but not joy. Joy comes out of pure love and respect for your beloved. A spoonful of lust can dissolve all the knowledge of the world in it. Life thus becomes meaningless. Make love as if you are worshiping God. Make love as if you are sacrificing everything. Make love as if there is no life or death, good or evil, heaven or earth and man or woman.'

To delight them Padmini told a story:

"Madri waited for her husband Pandu who had gone for a long hunting trip. Her body was full of vitality to welcome her husband into her bedroom. The thought of her husband made her private parts moist with love. Her husband's other wife was known for her courage and wisdom. She was a legendary figure who was destined to be remembered for eternity. However, Madri was a simple girl whose only possession was her natural beauty. Madri talked like a young girl and not like a queen. Her friends were normal peasant girls. She had bathed in milk and decorated her bedroom with flowers, clothes, paintings and jewels. Her husband came with a sad expression on his face. Pandu had accidentally shot a sage who wore deerskin. The sage cursed him with death the moment he makes love. The husband and wife looked at each other with love but death himself was standing between them. His other wife had a boon from a sage who presented her with five mantras. The moment one of the mantra is uttered a god will come from heaven and make love to the one uttering the mantra and bestow a child upon her. The childbirth will happen without pains just after the god has finished making love and the virginity knot shall be restored. So is the work of the divine. The other wife with her husband's permission uttered three mantras and three boys were born. The other wife had used the first mantra before her marriage. That is a different story. Since the wife was not selfish and jealous, she gave the last mantra to Mandri. The twin gods made love to Madri and two sons were born to her. The experience of being one with god is the greatest experiences of all. Madri still valued to love of her beloved over all. Everyday she would wait for her husband to make love to her knowing well that it is not going to happen. Years passed. She and her husband grew in wisdom. All the treasures of the world were nothing to them. Pandu came close to Madri and talked to her with love as usual. They looked at each other's eyes. They wanted each other. Even death cannot stop them. They made love out of wisdom. Their lovemaking was greater than the love making of the gods. Pandu smiled out of joy and died. Madri was heart broken. When her husband was being cremated she entered through the doors of fire to be one with her husband."

When God came that night Padmini just hugged him and said, 'A small hug out of love is much stronger than hours of love making. A small smile of a childlike mind soothes the infinite soul as nothing else can. Men seek refuge in complex obscure philosophies but salvation lies in truths like "God is love" and "Be happy and make others happy". Men can't accept the simplicity of life and go after mystic obscurities.'

Padmini wondered about the divine words that came out of her mouth with awe and surprise. 'Did the Divine One put these words in my mouth?' she wondered.

They slept that night in each other's arms.

42

When Padmini woke up, she heard a chaos outside the temple. She walked with pride towards the crowds. God was tied to a wooden pole.

'We found this cursed low caste man near your temple. His father was the one who masturbated over your idol years ago and cursed the village. What punishment shall we give him?' asked the high priest.

'Leave him in the jungle'

'O! Holiness! He is the banished one. His mother dared to speak against our laws and escaped into the forest. He should be beheaded'

'I know that but the torture of loneliness that he is going to experience in the jungle is greater that any of your punishments. He should be left inside the jungle. It is destiny.'

'So be it. O Holy One!'

Padmini decided to go into the jungle in search of God who did not visit her for two months after this incident.

43

Padmini talked about love and death to the people as if it meant the same. Padmini tried hard to control the destructive fire that was burning inside her. In a scorching hot night, Padmini swam into the forest from her chamber. She searched for him as if she was searching for a lost child. She felt a kind of weakness she had never felt before. The darkness was fading but Padmini was still emotionally blind. She stepped on a thorn bush. She was bleeding. She could hear steps. She was glad to know it was God.

'God!' she said bluntly.

'Did you step on those thorns? They killed my mother.'

'God! We will meet in heaven. Goodbye earth and its prejudices.'

Padmini closed her eyes. It was God's turn to hear steps. God carried Padmini and threw her into the thorny bush. More blood.

The people who saw this killed God and let his body to rot.

'God is dead. We are now just pieces of matter. Let's kill ourselves.' said an old priest.

'God will never die!' said a powerful voice. The people trembled. It was Padmini. The thorns could not poison her.

'The divine radiance is not in my body but in my soul. Your beliefs are weak. Your ideas are rotten. You are murderers. I am leaving my body. I am going to the heavens. Do not stop me.'

Padmini looked at God's body. It was rotting. Padmini kissed it. She kissed it again and again. Her hunger and thirst had made her blind of his ugly odours. Her dry lips kissed and kissed until it no longer could kiss. Starvation killed her.

44

Dominic looked into himself. He was a woman; he was a man. He waited in his chair for his name to be called. He talked to the people sitting near him with enthusiasm; they loved listening to him. He waited for his chance with a peaceful patience.

Since the exams were closer, only a few participated for the competitions. Dominic won the first prize for dance and the second prize for singing. Dominic was not proud; it was a kind of tranquillity.

45

ACT TWO

Chorus:

Words flew from the Novelist like nuclear missiles.

Words spilled like blood.

Words hurt people who wore coats and suits.

Is it Guilt or Joy, which lies hidden in the mind?

[Enter Novelist with a pen covered with a condom. Dominic is trying to cover his nakedness with a book. If the English dictionary is not available, use a history textbook.]

Novelist: The stories of sad women talk more to the soul than the stories of sad men. Religions, cultures, languages, laws and dogmas are like the words of the Priestess. They follow you to your grave. We are all slaves to our times; our bodies make love according to its tick-tocks. Our ancestors have moulded culture and tradition with their rough bare hands; we are now facing the burden of their cultural sins. Forget about men who look at women as sex objects, women themselves are taught by the society to see their own bodies as sex objects. Women look at their own bodies with shame and dishonour; they do not realise that their bodies are God's masterpieces. They do not realise the divine power inside their bodies that has made humans survive for millions of years facing the deadliest of obstacles. I personally do not like the use of sex to sell art but how else can I make money. Readers go hunting for it between pages. I need to put it somewhere. I do not like people who make sex public saying, 'The world is my witness, and I am having good sex' or 'I fuck, therefore

I am.' Sex should always happen peacefully behind a lock. Sex should be a natural reaction between two individuals that brings them together in love. Sex is not the hundred and two positions, which appears in the book 'How to have great sex?' Sex in this novel is artificial and unrealistic. If you have sex like Padmini and God, you may break your bones. Lustful readers see only the sex scenes in my novel. Knowledgeable readers see only the reason in my novel. The reader of wisdom sees the soul in my novel.

Dominic: Stop it! You are the world's worst pornographer. Your novel is the worst novel ever written. The dialogues are unreal. You expect every reader to be a sex-starved teenager. It is just uncontrolled guy lit. Giving multiple dimensions to my life will take you nowhere. Your philosophy has its own loopholes. The sex scenes you create enter into the unconscious mind of good readers and create negative energies that will come into the surface and destroy the world with lust. A teenager recently committed suicide trying to imitate a scene from a movie. What would he have done if he starts reading this book? Porn makes adults do the same. An artist spent years in his office room painting masterpieces. One fine day, he stepped out and witnessed an accident. A young girl was bleeding to death. The artist could not tell the difference between blood and paint. He let the girl die. Dear, Sappho Dionysus, you are that artist and your readers will become like you too. They will not be able to distinguish between reality and fiction. They will see everything through the perverted cooling glass of lust. The world they see will be filled with bodies that could be exploited. Their eyes will be burning with lascivious passions. The mention of the word 'rape' can give any humane person a bad day and you have repeated the word so many times. Some words pollute the mind. They make us forget great words like love, kindness and hope. Such words should not be written. I am trying to give you good advice.

Novelist: Thank You! When I create a paradise, should I not also create the tree of knowledge with a serpent on it? Ow! Where was I? Yes, The number 46.

46

The rich man has the Multi-national company.

The middle-class man has his B. Tech job.

The poor man had none.

The rich woman has her feminism.

The middle-class woman has her education.

The poor woman has none.

The rich child has the silver spoon.

The middle-class child has the cartoon network.

The poor child has heaven waiting for him. (Written on the walls of an Engineering college)

—Dominic Rodrigues

25/12/2009

47

Dominic watched Manju talking to a few boys. He felt jealous. He felt as if they were his enemies. He later felt ashamed of himself. He wanted her very badly. He imagined himself making love to her. Dominic had committed adultery with his eyes. He always thought about Manju, her smile, her dimples and her voice. His brain could chew on deepening feelings of love for hours together. 'Is this really love?' he wondered. He had one and a half years more in Assissi. He had time to decide.

48

Dominic touched her hands and said, 'I do not know how will you react to this, but I love you. This might be a feeling that many people have felt. I feel my love is true . . .'

'I love you'

They held their hands and smiled at each other with joy.

Dominic decided to join the army. His uniform made him look just like an army man. Dominic had his first chance to kill his enemies. He looked wicked. He shot a bullet and killed an enemy. Another enemy ran towards him with a knife. The knife entered him. He managed to shoot the second enemy. They all fell onto the ground.

A woman entered with a white shawl over her head and sat near Dominic's body.

'My love!' she said, 'I loved you. But what did you love?'

Another woman entered with a white shawl and sat near the first enemy's body.

'My hero!' she said, 'Were you really brave?'

The third woman entered and sat near the body of the second enemy.

'My son!' she said, 'Your father's lust has faded away. Am I your real mother?'

The women threw their white shawls, untied their hair and picked up black shawls. They raised it into the air shouting and screaming with a spirit of revolution—

'Fair is foul, and foul is fair,

Fair is the hag with filthy hair'

The director said, 'Good Witches! You were magnificent. Dominic and Hassan try to be more flexible on stage. Our modern Macbeth is ready to enter. Let's have some lime tea.'

Manju came near Dominic and said, 'Dude, You did well! I loved the way you fell down. Did you hurt your bums? You looked cool.'

'All hot girls are, paradoxically, cool.' thought Dominic.

'There is only one sin—Not to Love. There is only one virtue—Love. There is only one puzzle—Love. There is only one religion—Love', said Professor Joseph as an introduction to the play 'Anthony and Cleopatra'. The sleeps of the students were disturbed. 'Love', the Professor continued, 'is a highly misunderstood word. When I once asked a priest on what the ultimate aim of a human life should be he said, "To love and be loved."In addition, another priest said "To make the life of at least one person happy by filling his or her life with love". I love you. I love my dog. I love Facebook. I love nude women. I love Rajinikant. Does 'love' really mean 'love'? Can the signifier ever represent the signified? What most of you feel is just infatuation. A trick played by your hormones. A flame that goes out when the candle is eaten up. True love happens only after years of experience. A true lover follows the four C's—Confidence, Commitment, Conscience and Creativity (writes on the board). A true lover does not fall in love but rises in love. Read my latest book on true love. It is available in the college store. In the play . . . ' The students' psychological sleep was not disturbed.

49

'Let's all join together and revolt against the hostel administration which treats us as slaves,' said Dominic, 'If everybody decides to stand outside during the study time and shouts how you think the administration can control us?'

'Do you know the difficulties I went through to get an admission in this hostel? What do you think our parents will think about us?' asked Justine.

'Just a few months of boot-licking and we can go out as free birds.' said Mike.

'We should not be selfish. We must think about our juniors.' replied Dominic.

Shabri stood up and said, 'The equality which you believe in is a myth. There is no equality in this world. There are no human rights. Idealistic dreams always remain as dreams. Who do you think is trying his best to preserve the environment in spite of so many warnings from climate experts? Everybody wants to beat others and become successful. Is money the ultimate goal of life?'

More confusion flowed into the room. Dominic was disappointed.

50

[Continued from 9] Every man's self is locked up inside his skull; he is lonely. I kept secrets. I hid facts. I hid the photos of cricketers in an old jar, which no one is going to open. My aunts brought me presents. I tried to remember the face of my uncle James who went missing. He had presented a toy robot on my third birthday. I still keep it safely. Uncle loved a girl and called her Rosy. She wore a white frock with red roses painted on it. She wore a rose on her thick black hair. Her lips looked like a rose. However, uncle was allowed to kiss only the rose on her hair. One day she allowed him to kiss her lips. Uncle was promised another kiss before she left. She died of fever and Uncle did not want to marry. When his best friend cheated him after his retirement, he told me that if he had decided to marry he would have got a girl more rosy than Rosy. My uncle told good stories about beautiful women who were actually yakshis, ghosts, angels, fairies, demons or tree spirits. It happened to all women in the stories told by men. I loved my uncle and was very upset when he left us without saying a word. I did not like to go out and play cricket like other boys. I listened to Boney M and Michael Jackson who were my dad's favourites. I listened to the stories my father told me in which every character had a magical pet dog. The masters are always in danger while the pet dogs keep on rescuing them. In the end, the pet dogs give up their lives to save their good masters. The masters were godlike. The pet dogs were humanlike. My mother often told tales about girls and boys without parents who roam around the towns and the cities only to be cheated, kidnapped, adopted and punished. Did they find out the truth about their parents? Did they complete their schooling? Did they become millionaires? Did they get married? Did they die? Ask my mother. My aunt told a story about a dark boy who saves the life of a proud fair boy. I never stole the 'Fair and Lovely' cream from my aunt's table; my mother did. My Grandmother told me a modern day story of a saint who possessed the combined qualities of Dominic Savio and Francis of Assisi. 'Who is that saint?' I asked my Grandmother. 'That saint is you.

You should become a saint. Grandma will be very happy.' I attended a wedding and wanted to dance with all the small girls. I fell in love with a girl in a blue dress. Blue was my favourite colour. When I was younger green was my favourite colour until I saw an Onida advertisement in which the devil wore a green dress. I fell in love with a girl who refused to talk to me after I failed in my Maths test. I loved girls with round faces. I used to compare their faces to that of the moon. I had troubles learning multiplication tables. All the people around me tried their best to teach me multiplication tables. They were unsuccessful. A new Headmistress came and tried her best with a cane to teach me the tables. Her cane taught me how to tie my shoelace. She sometimes did not let me go home and once said, 'I will exchange your head with your mother's. Your mother is an M.Sc in Mathematics.' I spend two days thinking about such a situation. The Headmistress died of cancer but I think she died out of her disappointment as a teacher of the multiplication tables. 'Did she have the cane with her when they buried her?' asked my sister Faustina. My sister was allowed to go for bharathanatiyam dance classes but I was not. I watched her steps from a distance and started learning them. When my mother gave us glasses of milk, I would wait for my younger sister to finish her milk and would exchange the glasses. My mother would come from the kitchen and scold my sister for not drinking her milk. My sister became healthier. When I later remembered this incident, a Haiku came into my mind:

A glass of milk on a black tablecloth;

Spilled droplets seen:

The Moon and the Stars.

Boys used to bully me for being silent. I wished I were a girl. If I were a girl, I would not get beatings from other boys. They would only give me roses and I would give them slaps. I always sat on the same chair before the same boring academic book reading or studying. Studying was the nightmare that destroyed my childhood. Dominic Rodrigues will not study. He hates it. But, what to do mother is stranding with a stick.[To be continued]

51

Dominic tried his best sending text messages to Manju that oscillated between friendship and love. Two philosophies tortured him.

Philosophy One: I am in love with Manju because our souls were destined to merge. That is why no other girl enters my mind.

Philosophy Two: Manju and me have a lot of differences—religion, beliefs, social interaction, philosophy of life etc. How can we live together?

52

Manju gave Dominic a story titled 'The Three Dildos' and asked Dominic to play the critic.

THE THREE DILDOS—Manju

When Adam and Eve went hunting, a red flower distracted Eve. She touched it and felt something going through her veins. Adam threw a huge stone on an animal. The cry of the animal before it feel dead hurt Eve in some way. Empathy was born. The divine quality descended into earth from the heart of God. Adam's hand that was red with blood held Eve. 'Do not cry. I love you.' said he, 'Now I can give the animal a name.' Adam was the first zoologist. He spends most of the time naming animals, birds and plants. Eve saw everything as a single whole.

Eve washed her stained hand and thought about the sin Adam had committed. God had told them not to hunt. She put her hands into the mud and discovered a seed. She planted it and from the seed came a tree full of fruits. She ate a fruit and threw the seed. Again from the new seed a new tree was born. Agriculture was born.

'We do not have to hunt any more. We shall plant seeds and eat the fruits which as the gifts of God.' said she to Adam. Adam's ego that had born out of sin could not accept the fact that Eve had discovered agriculture. Adam took the stone with which he had killed the animal and warned that he would kill her. Eve obeyed. Thus, she had sinned.

Adam took the stone and wrote history—

Adam felt lonely. He was always masturbating thinking of a being like himself. He did not know why he was doing this. God knew why. God created Eve. Adam went close to Eve and felt her warmth. Adam touched Eve all over her body. Eve also touched Adam. They kissed each other passionately. They felt happy. They loved each other. They found food for each other. When Adam went into her, there was pleasure and no pain. They were the first kissers and the first love makers. They never questioned, scolded or envied each other. They wee always patient and kind. They prayed together. One day Eve went near the forbidden tree. Something attracted her towards the tree. Two eyes hypnotized her from a distance. She saw a serpent that had the hands and legs of a man. 'Make love to me.', said the serpent. 'No.', replied Eve, 'But how come you have the hands and legs of a man?' 'Because I ate that fruit', said the serpent. Eve was about to leave when the serpent asked, 'Do you want to experience a different kind of pleasure—a pleasure greater than the one Adam give you.' Eve agreed. The serpent sexually covered Eve. The serpent put its head into Eve's chalice. Its forked tongue grew hotter and explored into the depths. Eve opened her mouth unable to bear the burden of pleasures. The serpent put a fruit into her mouth. The taste of the fruit filled Eve's mind with a sense of pride. The serpent disappeared. Eve was left heart-broken. Eve wanted Adam to feel the same pleasure and thus gave some fruit for him to taste. Eve told her story to Adam. 'Can you make love to me like the serpent?' she asked. Adam said 'No' and was disappointed. Adam cried. 'Why did you make me eat the forbidden fruit? Why did you cheat me? How come you are so lucky?' Adam felt a pain in his throat that originated from his heart. It was the first case of heart attack. Adam and Eve started decorating their bodies with flowers and twigs to look more attractive to each other. God came and scolded them for plucking flowers and twigs and hurting his creation. They began blaming each other. They wanted to hurt each other. They made lust. The serpent who was actually the devil turned love into lust.

Cain who read and heard about history changed it according to his personal beliefs. His son who did not believe blindly in everything that his father said changed the story again. History changed as people changed. Eve plucked the red flower and told about her sufferings to it. It patiently heard until it died into brownness. Meanwhile Adam made three dildos to torture Eve when he is unable to torture her. They were called patriarchy, tradition and money.

53

Handsome, Hearty, Horny, He

Soft, Sexy, Sensible, She

Heavy, Hulky, Hemingway, He

Silent, Spiritual, Sappho, She

Hostile, Healthy, Hardware, He

Sporty, Spirited, Software, She

Hilarious, Honourable, Hero, He

Savage, Seductive, Sweetheart, She

Horrendous, Hazardous, Harasser, He

Sympathetic, Sceptical, Saviour, She

Hooligan, He

Spontaneous, She

Humanitarian, He

Supernatural, She

She made love to He.

He made love to She.

She was He

And He was She.

[When you read this poem for the second time convert 'He' into 'She' and 'She' into 'He'.]

(Written on a bench)

—Dominic Rodrigues

30/01/2009

54

'Good story,' said Dominic, 'but the names of the three dildos sound odd. I feel they are one with the stereotype feminist notions. I do not mean to hurt your beliefs but I think that the world is already interpreting the story of origin in thousand different ways according to the changing beliefs, cultures and values. Anyway, what's your next story about?'

'About a woman named Jesus who had to dress like a man in order to proclaim herself as God.'

'Jesus is a feminine male just like Krishna. But making him a female is not a good idea.'

'Why?'

'Do you know the story of how he chased traders from the temple?'

'The feminine nature should sometimes do that to attain their goals. Masculinity is a drop in the ocean of femininity. Sometimes a drop is a lot. I am also planning to write a story about the Samaritan woman who had five husbands and her erotic adventures. Her chaste dalliance with Jesus will also be a theme.'

'Are you going to write anything that is not an erotica?'

'Yes, I am going to write an alternative version of the Second World War. All Germen women decide to stop their men from going for the war and the world realises the power of women and give them absolute freedom.'

'All the wars in history were started by men: is it this you want to say? What about Helen of Troy and Joan of Arc?'

'They were forced into war by greedy men.'

'So World War II does not take place?'

'It takes place in the minds of humanity.'

They smiled.

55

Little drops of Infatuation

And little grains of Affection

Makes the mighty Love

And the God above.(Written on the walls of a famous monument)

—Dominic Rodrigues

01/01/2009

56

Dominic looked at the gothic chapel that was painted black with age. It had been weeks since he had attended mass. Dominic started to think the church as a capitalist institution that sold religious hope. Dominic thought, 'What is life if there is no life after death? What is god? Is he the petrol that energises the universal engine or is he the engine itself? Is it the word 'dog' spelled backwards? Why aren't women allowed to celebrate mass? Why can I not celebrate the mass instead of that old priest who does not know anything about the present day world? Why do some people say—We will go to heaven and others will not—just because they think that they are god's chosen people? Why people who call themselves godly are killing each other? Who are the gods and who are the devils? The works of the human psychology—Is that an answer?'

He stayed away from the church.

57

After Dominic collected the prize for the dance and singing competitions, he thought of preparing for his final examinations that will help him to get out of Assisi. He felt confident. He looked at the gothic chapel painted white after the renovation. He decided to go to church after nine months. He shared things with god. When the church bells tolled, he thought of the times he was called Immanuel.

58

The eleven-year-old Immanuel looked at the silver dagger he got as a gift on his eighth birthday from his father. He could feel some kind of energy coming from the dagger. The sharpness of the dagger pierced into his tiny finger causing tiny red drops to fall onto the ground. Immanuel did not feel the pain.

He had not seen his father for three years. He hid himself from his mother and talked to the dagger, 'You are my best friend. Teach me how to become like my father. I want to fight in the battle and kill many bad people. Will you help me?'

The only person he loved in the world was his infant brother who only knew to smile and cry. He dreamed about the great adventures he will have with his brother. When his brother's hand held his finger, he felt as if the wound was healing.

He could hear loud voices coming from a distance. He saw people coming towards his town on horsebacks. He saw his father raising his sword in the air as the hero of his dreams.

'Father! Father!' he cried. The father and his friends came closer.

'Father, I have a new brother. He looks just like me. Come and see.'

The father was shocked. All his fellow soldiers stared at him.

'Who is greater than your family?' they asked.

'Emperor Herod is.' replied the father.

'Who is greater than God?' they asked.

'Emperor Herod.' replied the father.

'Who is greater than love, fear, hope and friendship?'

'It is our saviour Emperor Herod.'

'Who is above all?'

When the father confidently said, 'The king is above all!' the soldiers cheered him up. The father walked into his own house crying, 'Long live King Herod!' All the people around him made noises of cheer by banging their swords on their shields. The mother cried, 'No! No!' Some soldiers whispered about the foolishness of women. The father killed his son and Immanuel lost his only brother.

59

'Father is the devil. He is a murderer.' cried Immanuel.

'No, son,' said the mother, 'It is King Herod who killed your brother. He has ordered to kill all children below the age of two. Your father is a soldier and he should obey the king.'

In the night when Immanuel was forced into sleep, the silver dagger woke him up. He quietly entered into his father's chamber. The father was naked over the mother convincing her, 'Let us have another son.'

The dagger entered into the father. Immanuel watched the blood thickening on the dagger as he ran. He wondered why his mother did not scream. *Did it make her happy? Did she die? Will she live for a hundred years after her husband's death?*

60

His feet took him to another town. He secretly entered into houses and watched how men controlled their women at night. He wanted muscles like the wrestlers in his dreams who broke the bones of men and made women beg on his legs. One day he decided to become a blacksmith. He wanted to learn more about weapons. He wanted to kill Herod. A blacksmith put his hand on Immanuel's shoulder seeing a strange kind of courage in his eyes. Immanuel worked days and nights for the blacksmith.

'From this day onwards can I call you my son?' asked the blacksmith.

'Yes.', replied Immanuel. The blacksmith's eyes were in tears. Immanuel was emotionless.

'Look at these people out there!' said the blacksmith, 'They are the rich and the famous. They either starve or kill the poor. If you want to be successful, you should either rob them or kill them. Some call them Romans and others call them devils. Some cowards wear Roman clothes and call themselves rich. All of them should be killed. You should kill them. The world is full of objects—objects with less value or objects with greater value. Gold, silver, weapons, food, women and nature are all objects. Those who learn how to control these objects become God.'

Immanuel asked Joseph, the blacksmith's son who was older to him, 'Do you know what God uses as a weapon?'

Joseph's answers did not satisfy Immanuel.

'It is a silver dagger.' said Immanuel.

Immanuel left the blacksmith's house without informing anyone. The blacksmith scolded his son and cursed him. He tore his clothes and shaved his head. He did not work. Instead, he stood by the door waiting for Immanuel for months. Joseph felt helpless. He tried his best doing his father's job. He could not earn as his father did. He sometimes sobbed thinking of his mother.

One day as the blacksmith was sitting by his door contemplating suicide Joseph saw Immanuel coming from a distance.

'Father!' cried Joseph, 'Immanuel has returned.'

The blacksmith jumped with joy and hugged Immanuel. Immanuel looked fresh and healthy. The muscles of his body moved like fishes caught in a net. He now resembled the wrestler of his dreams. There was a noticeable change in the way he behaved and spoke. He behaved as if he had some kind of authority over others. The blacksmith did not ask him why he left or what he did during the long period of absence.

61

Immanuel along with Joseph entered a rich man's house. They filled their bags with riches. When they were about to leave they saw that the rich man's daughter was awake. Joseph's heart started to beat with fear. Immanuel went closer to the girl. He looked at the girl's eyes. He kissed her. The girl's sister woke up. Immanuel could see jealousy in her eyes. He kissed her too.

Immanuel and Joseph were counting the money along with the blacksmith. 'You have found the keys to a woman's heart', the blacksmith whispered to Immanuel, 'Use it!'

Pious priests stoned the rich man's daughters to death after they were found to be pregnant.

Many houses were robbed and many women were stoned because of Immanuel.

'Leave the women alone. We may get into problems', said Joseph.

'Women like men were never meant to be alone. I sink them into the sea of loneliness.' replied Immanuel to a confused Joseph, 'If a woman wants to scream let her scream, but if her scream would kill me I better stop her scream. I am the rider and she is my horse. My travel will never end.'

Immanuel always carried a black cloth with which he would shut the woman's mouth before raping her. Since they did not scream when they were being deflowered they were stoned to death according to Jewish laws.

62

Immanuel loved Joseph, as he was his only companion. He found Joseph to be a fool. The words that Joseph spoke did not make any sense to Immanuel.

'I don't like hurting people but I am forced into it. I am going to quit. From henceforth I will remain a truthful blacksmith following all the rules', said Joseph.

Donkeys do not mind being slaves as long as it gets something to eat. Can Joseph become like a donkey?

63

Immanuel made many friends. In the beginning, he talked to them about women. Then he talked about the ways one can torture women. Then he talked about the different types of weapons. He talked about the uses of wealth and weapons. He talked about the objects of the world. Later he started speaking about the wicket Roman Empire. He spent days talking about some kind of revolution which Joseph could not understand. He won friends. He won enemies. However, all were faithful listeners of Immanuel.

64

Immanuel and his friends were drinking together and planning how to kill a rich man when a servant came running towards him shouting, 'Immanuel! The wine you just drank was the one that was poisoned.' Immanuel fell onto the ground. He was breathing heavily. The friends made him lie on his bed and discussed how to go on with their plans without Immanuel.

When Immanuel woke up fresh the next day the servant cried, 'A miracle! A miracle!'

'I must be God to survive that poison', said Immanuel to his friends. His friends began to believe so.

65

Immanuel was in the wilderness. He thought about the wild animals that could attack him. He was brave. He held his silver dagger more tightly and raised it into the air. The sky strangely became dark and bright as if the sun disappeared and appeared continuously. The clouds looked strange. Lights belonging to unknown colours poured out from them. Soft angelic music filled the air. Echoes of sounds silenced the angelic one. The colourful lights danced to the echoes. He heard a strong masculine voice from heaven, 'You are the messiah who is born to save the people. You are the messiah of whom the prophets talked about.'

Immanuel found himself in a deserted town among thousands of dead soldiers. The atmosphere had the smell of blood. The voice was heard once more.

'God felt bored in heaven. He has come to earth for enjoyment. He has come to punish the wicked and the foolish with the power of pain. He has taken the form of a human weapon.'

Silver daggers just as the one Immanuel was holding fell from the skies and pierced into the dead soldiers. Blood started pouring out of them like fountains. The deserted town soon became into a river of blood. Immanuel was standing on a Roman shield that floated over the river. The shield started spinning. Immanuel could not bear it. He felt weightless. He felt as if he was flying in the air.

When the shield stopped spinning Immanuel was in a cave filled with giant fireflies of various colours, naked screaming women and mermaids struggling for water. Some mermaids had golden tails and silver hair and other ones had silver tails with golden hair. When the screaming women cried, the mermaids tried to drink the tears. The hairs of the screaming women were so long that it looked like black streams that were flowing against each other. Immanuel waited for a long time for the voice but the voice said nothing.

Immanuel woke up from his dream. His hand was full of blood because he had held the silver dagger that lay close to him too tightly.

66

'Immanuel, I saw the messiah talking from a mountain top.' said Joseph to a surprised Immanuel. 'How do you know that he is the messiah? The Romans might be playing a trick on us.'

'From the way he spoke I could understand that he is the messiah. He spoke about the importance of love and kindness. He treated men and women equally and allowed his women disciples to express their views on his teaching. He played with children whole-heartedly and asked us to do the same. He spoke about the importance of being humble and simple. He told us never to feel anger and hatred towards anyone. He spoke ill about the rich and the powerful. He said the one could not serve God and wealth at the same time. God is above all worldly riches.'

'How foolish you are, Joseph? How can one live without wealth? This must be a trick played by the Romans.'

'It is not a trick. Come with me and you will know the truth. I am going to get married to one of his followers called Martha.'

67

'You should see other human beings as parts of your own body. When people hurt you, it is just God testing your patience', said Martha to Joseph in a very sweet voice. She came closer to him and kissed him. They started making love.

Immanuel who was secretly hiding and watching them came forward and pushed Martha from Joseph. He showed her a long black cloth and asked, 'Do you remember this?'

Martha was silent. Joseph tried to push Immanuel out of the room but Immanuel gave a hard blow on Joseph's shoulder and threw him towards the ground.

'You are the same Martha I saw making lust to one of Herod's servants.' said Immanuel in an angry mood, 'I remember you saying to the women who mocked you—Woman of the world respect me, the whore, for it is because of me you are not being raped everyday. You were very young then. I wanted to destroy you even then. You have not lost your baby like face. Are you still whoring yourself to the Roman's even now? Are they the ones who saved you from those Jewish priests? I poisoned Herod to death, I raped you in the streets, and now you have come again with a false messiah to seduce my best friend from me—'

Joseph got up, pushed Immanuel onto the ground, and tied him up to a pole. Joseph wanted to hit Immanuel but Martha prevented him from doing it.

Martha then spoke to Immanuel, 'It is true. I was a slave in the hands of the Romans. Just like any other woman, I was a slave to lustful men. You think that woman loved to be raped and tortured. You are being blinded by the same society that blinded people for generations. I was going to be stoned by the same Jewish priests who you ran away from. No one came to save me. Not even the Romans. Then came a man who asked the person who has not sinned in his life to throw the first stone on me. All of them left. I saw the image of God in his face. I realised that he is the messiah. I followed him. I worshiped him. He taught me the scriptures. When we are able to love God, we can find love everywhere. Reasons and emotions may make you struggle for the truth. In the process, you hurt people and you hurt God. We should struggle for truth with love, worship and faith in God and only then, you can forgive as I have forgiven you. You should also change your ways and meet the messiah.'

'I am the messiah. I am God. Women have no place in the temple of God. They should not be allowed to worship. Scriptures in the hands of women will forever be defiled. Your punishment will be great.' shouted Immanuel as Joseph and Martha left the place.

68

When Joseph was walking in the street at night after successfully completing his work an old drunkard stopped him saying, 'Do you remember me? You were the one who along with your friend raped my two daughters and stole all my wealth. You killed my daughters and now I am going to kill you.' The old man took out his dagger and came close to Joseph.

'Don't do this.' requested Joseph, 'Please forgive me!'

Joseph pushed the man and began to run. The old man followed him shouting out war cries. Immanuel came out from behind a bush and stabbed the old man to death without listening to Joseph's protests.

'Do you know your father died because of him', said Immanuel.

Joseph was silent.

'I saved your life. Now you may realise that I am God. You are also my instrument. The whole of humanity thinks Herod died of sickness. I poisoned him to death with the poisonous herb you showed me on the day we met for the first time. Eve has possessed Martha. We can cure her and she can join us. Tell her that I will make her a queen and she will surely forget her old messiah. I was born to destroy Rome. I was born to become a king. Can I ask you a favour, Joseph?'

All of a sudden, many men started to come out their hiding places. Joseph was surprised seeing their numbers.

'These are my angels. Take them to your father's land and camp them there.'

Joseph could do nothing to escape from the situation.

'What are you going to do?' asked Joseph to the camping men.

'We are going to destroy Rome. We are going to attack Pilate.'

69

Martha was alone in the street waiting for Joseph. He had asked her to wait. She dreamed about the new life that she is going to live. She wanted to say many things to the messiah when she meets him. She noticed a few shadows moving behind her. A hand came from behind and caught hold of her neck. She felt helpless and fainted.

When Martha woke up, she found many men groping her body and sexually torturing her mercilessly. She saw Immanuel laughing at her being raped. Immanuel placed his leg on her chest and said, 'So here hides your messiah. Let me give him a massage with my legs.' Immanuel and his friends whipped her and spat on her. In the end, Immanuel took his silver dagger and poked her abdomen. Blood and water started to flow from her wound. Martha said, 'Forgive them O Lord' and gave up the spirit. Joseph knew nothing of this incident.

Joseph questioned Immanuel about the way he treats women and talked about the messiah who proclaims equal rights for men and women.

Immanuel got up and said before everybody, 'I rape women to destroy their evil pride, their false beauty, which questioned the divine beauty of man from the times of Adam and Eve. I kill and rob people to gather men and weapons to form the divine army that is going to save the God's chosen people from the Romans and lead them to the land of milk and honey.'

'What is the use? When you become the ruler of Rome, you will be no different from the Romans. You will kill and you will rape. Any army on earth is the army of Beelzebub.' shouted Joseph.

Immanuel asked his men to tie up Joseph and said, 'I will give you a day's time. If you do not change your mind my silver dagger will do its work.'

70

Immanuel swam in a golden sea. The sun was red and the sky was blue. The silver clouds changed its shape to depict a war between humans and animals. The animals destroyed the humans with their silver horns, which easily broke the silver shields of the humans, and then turned into humans and fought against each other. The battle became more and more complex. The silver clouds completely covered the sun and the blue sky. The thunder sounded loud and strange but there was not lightening in the sky. Slowly all the clouds faded and the sun was red and the sky was purely blue.

Immanuel could swim no longer. The golden sea swallowed him. Immanuel found himself in a palace filled with diamonds. He moved his hands towards the diamonds when a woman who was nine feet tall caught hold of him and talked to him in a language he could not understand. She castrated him. He screamed as everything became dark. A voice that resembled the voice of Immanuel's mother said, 'You think you are God. You are just a mortal who is proud of your God given sexuality. You think that all the women of the world are yours just because God has made you virile. You shall be born in this world again as Padmini. You will then know the meaning of what I am speaking.'

Immanuel found himself on a giant rock. He noticed that the ants were bigger than him. They chased him. He became so small that he could see atoms that were much bigger than he was. The voice from his earlier dream said, 'You are not God. Look how small you are. The castles of your pride are nothing before the largeness of the universe. No being is greater than another being. No nation is greater than another nation. No belief is greater than another belief. No dream is perfect. No dream is false. Perfection can be attributed only to God. Men in order to satisfy their lust and greed twist ritual, belief, religion, culture, nature, thinking to suit their own needs; this takes them far away from the ultimate Truth. You will suffer.'

'Who are you?' asked Immanuel.

'I am your voice. I am your soul.'

When Immanuel woke up from his dream, he found himself surrounded by Roman soldiers. They castrated him and gave him a wooden cross to carry. When Immanuel looked around, he could see Joseph carrying a similar cross. His friends were spiting over him and shouting, 'Crucify the traitors.'

71

'The man who is being crucified with us is the messiah. He is the one who saved Martha from being stoned. He is dying on the cross for the sake of humanity. He is dying to protest against the hatred, violence and vengeance one human being showers over an other.' whispered Joseph to Immanuel.

'No one is the messiah. No one is God. All are slaves to fate. All are slaves to proud masters.' replied Immanuel. Joseph did not hear Immanuel's reply and as he was looking around for Martha. They were crucified to the cross.

Immanuel said, 'If you are the messiah save yourselves and us.'

The man who was crucified between them did not reply.

'Remember me in paradise.' said Joseph.

'You will be there with me in the paradise of God.' replied the messiah.

Immanuel tried to forget his pride. Immanuel wanted to ask for forgiveness for he had hurt both Joseph and the messiah. He saw a lamp that said, 'I will take away your darkness. All you have to do is come closer.' Immanuel went closer. ' . . . and closer and closer.' All the darkness in his heart evaporated into the light. The light was put out. He could not bear the pain when his legs were cut into pieces. He cried unto his death.

72

Dominic began to cry in the church thinking of the sins he had committed in his previous births. Dominic and Silence was the only people inside the church; maybe god was there too. His tears took away a big burden from his heart. The cold atmosphere and the marble flooring send cold waves throughout his body. Dominic emptied his mind while the cold waves made his body shiver. He decided to go with his friends to Marina beach and buy a gift for Fr. Ben.

73

'Fr. Ben, I don't like to be part of any religious activities. I believe that all the bad people in this world are bad because of their religious beliefs.'

'Dominic, that does not justify your behaviour. You do not talk to your friends and you spend most of your time alone. You should try to accept the society around you with all its merits and demerits.'

'When I am alone I am in paradise. When I am not alone, imperfect beings surround me. Humans are born to hate each other.'

'No human is perfect. We hurt the people we love. We hurt the people we hate. Minds cannot understand each other. Sometimes all that is true. Only a good communication facilitated by God can save humankind. Vivekandanda once said that people who think that others are sinners are sinners themselves. Rituals and customs may meaningless to our modern minds, but it brings people together to make that good communication.'

'Did you get that from one of those communication books?'

'Maybe'

Dominic felt comfortable speaking to Fr. Ben.

74

ACT THREE

Chorus:

Our two heroes travelled around the world.

Our two heroes read all the books.

Our two heroes lied like hell.

Our two heroes learned all the arts and sciences.

Our two heroes fought within their minds.

Our two heroes never changed opinions.

[Both the Novelist and Dominic are lying on the same bed and fighting for the bed sheet. The bed sheet should be a costly one.]

Dominic: I think you are obsessed with money and fame just like Immanuel. Are you writing this novel to propagate the philosophies you believe in?

Novelist: That is what all writers do. More philosophy means more problems. More problems mean more twists. More twists mean more publicity.

Dominic: You write rubbish. You have travelled a lot from your moon like condom concept that I find very metaphysical. Are you trying to tease me through this novel? Do you think you are practicing what you preach? Why don't you mind your own business instead of writing this stupid novel and making the whole world hostile towards you?

Novelist: I am writing a book on you because I love you. People today are very sad. I am going to make them happy by telling lies about you. A lie is the new truth. By travelling through the dark tunnel of lies, we discover the truth in the end. Good rubbish makes many people happy. I will keep on writing and no human can stop me.

Dominic: I love you too. It is all because Jesus who said, 'Love thy enemies.'

75

When I was in first standard, I asked my mother, 'Will you love me?'

'I will love you when you pass and go to second standard.' said she.

When I was in tenth standard, I asked my mother, 'Will you love me?'

'Study well and pass the examination.' said she.

When I completed my education, I asked my mother, 'Will you love me?'

'Get a good job and then I will.' said she.

When I got a job, I asked my mother, 'Will you love me?'

'Get me a daughter-in-law and I will' said she.

When I got married, I forgot my mother and made love to my wife.

When my wife felt lonely, she asked me, 'Will you love me forever?'

'Get me a child and I will love you forever.' said I.

She did not get a child who would latter ask, 'Will you love me?'

And breaking my promise I loved my wife forever.

—The Novelist

12/04/2005

76

[Continued from 50] My autobiography which is written solely to protest against a novel called *Rebirths* would not be perfect if I do not mention my romantic life with females, books and films in detail. I have mentioned some of those females in my life earlier but that is not all. I fell in love with the Principal's daughter. She looked cute when she scolded me. She went to another school and started scolding someone else. I loved a girl because she was fairer than any other girls in class were. She loved the boy who was fairer than other boys were and that was not I. I loved a girl because she was the only girl who talked to me in class. I loved a girl just because she loved the novel *Dracula* by Bram Stoker, which is my favourite. I loved a girl because she looked like the cute movie actor I saw on T.V. I loved a girl who sat close to me. I cried when I had to leave her after I passed my pre-degree examination. It is better to have loved and lost. I loved Manju. When I was not falling in love, I read books and watched movies. I started with Sherlock Holmes and Harry Potter in the beginning. I wanted to become an English teacher so that I could always read stories. I read *The God of small things* before joining for B.A. I read the novels of Sidney Sheldon. His *The Other Side of Midnight* is one of my favourites. I read *The Piano Teacher*. I was shocked when the sexually repressed daughter rapes her mother. If I become a writer, I would never shock people like that. I would never become like the writer of *Rebirths*. I watched the Harry Potter movies. I read *The Godfather* and then watched the movies based on it. That is when I decided to become a filmmaker. I fell in love with movies. They were more faithful than those girls were. I opened my mouth in awe when the red sea parted in *The Ten Commandments*. I did the same when I saw the chariot scene in *Ben-Hur*. I felt for the poor slaves in *Spartacus*. Though Spartacus was a slave the way he walked would humble the pride of the greatest of emperors. The theme music of *E.T*, *Jurassic Park*, *Titanic* and *Psycho* echoed in my heart for a million times. Charlie Chaplin made me laugh and cry at the same time. *Bobby* made in fall in love. *The Shawshank Redemption*, *The Artist*,

A.I and *The Terminal* made me cry out of joy. My heart felt slient over the simplicity of *Pather Panchali* and *Tokyo Story*. I re-watched movies like *The E.T*, *Ben-Hur*, *The Ten Commandments* and *The Sound of Music*. My list of my favourite movies is given below.

English—*Citizen Kane; The Godfather; The Godfather Part—3; The Shawshank Redemption; Schindler's List; Gone with the Wind; Ben-Hur; Dr. Zhivago; Lawrence of Arabia; Taxi Driver; City Lights; The Great Dictator; Gandhi; All Quiet on the Western Front; Psycho; Chinatown; The E.T; The Lord of the Rings: The fellowship of the ring; Carrie; A.I; Pulp Fiction; Requiem for a Dream; Borat.*

Indian—*The Apu Triology; Lagaan; Mathilukal; Goopy Gyne Bangha Byne; Mughal-e-azam; Awara; Bobby; Vishali; Piravi; Chemeen; Iruvar; Nayakan; Sholay; Kutty Srank; Dev D; Ee Adutha Kalathu; Ustad Hotel; Charulata; Nidra.*

Italian—*The Bicycle Thieves; Cinema Paradiso; La Dolce Vita; Eight and a half; Rome Open City; Life is Beautiful; Malena.*

French—*La Regle du Jeu; A Bout de Souffle; La Belle et la Bete; La Grande Illusion; Amelie*

Japanese—*Seven Samurai; Rashomon; Tokyo Story; Ran; Spirited Away; Godzilla; Ringu; Empire of Passion.*

German—*Metropolis; M; Run, Lola, Run; Downfall; Perfume: The story of a murderer; Das Boot; The Edge of Heaven; Nosferatu.*

Sorry, I cannot do justice to all the nations of the world. How can I forget Swedish movies like *The Seventh Seal* and *Persona*? How can I forget the Brazilian *City of God*? How can I forget the rising lion in the Russian *Battleship Potemkin*? Every nation makes unique kinds of movies that should not be compared with each other. I am not a great movie critic. Not everyone may love the movies that I love. Movies make me escape from the reality. They have taught me a lot. I am more interested in the philosophical part than the technical part. When I watched *Taxi Driver*, I realised that sex happens everywhere, in the television, magazines, books and internet, and not in real life. I lived among books and movies and not among human beings. Sometimes it is nice to be lonely. It is also true that people make you happy. We expect other people to make us happy especially the female ones if you are a male. I want to make people happy. But how can I? Here is an interesting list.

On Human Sexuality—*Lust, Caution; Empire of Passion; Kamasutra: A tale of true love; In the Realms of the Senses; King Kong; Psycho; Bliss; Sex and Zen; Samsara; The Last Temptations of the Christ; I like it Hot; Basic Instinct; The Blue Lagoon; The Lord of Files; Spilce.*

On Human Spirituality—*The Passion of Joan of Arc; The Last Temptations of the Christ; The Passion of the Christ; Ben-Hur; The Ten Commandments; Perfume: The story of a murderer; Naan Kadavul; Francis and Clare.*

I would like to take a break from movies and talk about the novelist. I dislike the novelist but I love him because he gives me company. If I had not spent hours fighting with words with the novelist I would die of boredom. May be I am the bad guy who always wanted to be the good guy. The novelist should not have written about me. [To be continued.]

77

'Awh! Look how beautiful is the shirt human's wear.'

Said a spider hanging in the air.

'I will make my version of it', he said like a bear.

The spider worked and did not care.

'Humans will know the greatness of spiders.' he thought.

'Web shirts will be the new fashion.' he thought.

After working for days,

The web shirt was made.

'Spiders are not asses.' Fathers would say he thought

After looking at his masterpiece,

He took rest hoping for the best.

A small boy came into the room

With his tiny broom.

He destroyed the spider's web shirt

And neatness came into the room.

The spider cried and cried.

He lost everything he dreamt of.

'Was not this boy a fan of Spider-man?' he thought

'Is this the way to treat the animal that inspired Spider-man?'

—The Novelist

24/12/2000

78

My father said, 'Go outside. Look into the hearts of people. You will know what they love and then go and write. Start writing now and never stop. Spin your story like a spider.' (Written in the personal diary)

—The Novelist

30/01/2000

79

Dominic wrote a story titled The Yakshi' and gave it to Manju as a gift.

THE YAKSHI

The people in Thamarapuram feared to venture into the forest nearby because they believed that a Yakshi lived there. Ask them if the Yakshi is a demi-god, a lonely spirit, a protector of trees or a protector of women and they would say, 'We know not. We know that she loves to dwell near Palm trees and Pala trees. We know that she looks very beautiful. We know that the sound of her anklet has seduced thousands of men. We know that she makes love to he victims. We know that she changes her form before eating up her victims. When she is not hungry, she would throw her victims into the Thamara stream. Do not go into the forest if you value your life.'

Grandmothers warned young children by telling stories about how the Yakshi killed children by drinking their blood. Teenage boys were told stories about lustful boys who was seduced by the smell of Pala trees and was finally consumed by the Yakshi. Husbands were told about how a man who cheated his wife was castrated and killed by the Yakshi. Woodcutters were told about a greedy woodcutter who was mutilated for cutting down a Pala tree. Peter Fernandez who came to investigate about the death of a British man called George Samuel loved to hear such stories though he did not believe in them. George Samuel was an ex-serviceman who was killed in Thamarapuram forest. His body was found floating in the Thamara stream. This incident made the legends of Thamarapuram more famous. Fernandez was an Anglo-Indian police officer who was known for his bravery. Fernandez decided to go into the forest all alone at night to prove to the world that the Yakshi is only a myth. According to him it is the extremist temple priest who is doing all this in order to make the people live in fear.

When Fernandez was getting ready to go into the forest, an elderly woman entered his room. Her hypnotic eyes prevented him from protesting. She said, 'Once an Anglo-Indian railway employee entered into this forest. He was a bachelor who loved stories about voluptuous deadly women. The full moon reflected on the magical Thamara pond and created a strange kind of light; the pink lotus in the pond mysteriously entwined the white lotus and made love like snakes. A black cobra began mating with a swan and a wolf with a lamp. The Bachelor saw a beautiful nude young woman sitting on one of the rocks in the pond and decorating her hair with red shoe flowers and basil leaves. A bed made of jasmine flowers was made beside the pond. She gently tapped her feet on a rock and music emerged from her anklet. Her behind was facing the bachelor. He observed the beauty of her backside with awe. It was so wide, wild and curvaceous that no human beauty could surpass it. Its slit looked like an entrance into heaven. Its glow was brighter than the sun. Its softness was more exotic than the bed of princess Thara. The moon felt jealous of its beauty. Her shape was that of a celestial vase that could hold the universe in it. Naturally, the bachelor lost all his self-control. He went closer to the young woman. When she turned and looked at him, he was blushing. Her look was tantalizing; her eyes looked innocent and passionate at the same time. When she winked, he felt as if her long eyelashes were calling him closer. Her lips that turned red and juicy made the same call. She willingly accepted him into her lap. He gifted her soft kisses and she gifted him softer ones. The kisses got wilder and wilder. She easily tore off his clothes with her nails that looked soft. Her animate hair started to carouse his body. Her tongue slithered throughout his body. He realised that she was the Yakshi yet, since lust knows no fear, he was lost in her. Her voluptuous hair grew longer and tied his hand behind his back. She began to dance violently with him. Her dance was more vibrant than any other human dance; the flexibility of her body would baffle even the greatest acrobats. It also looked more beautiful than any other dance. Nature stood in awe just to witness the cosmic dance. He wanted to stop but she did not let him stop. She danced jumping from one rock to another, flying over the foliage of trees and bouncing into the night clouds. Her breasts stabbed into his rib cage. Flesh devoured flesh and fluid devoured fluid. Her lips drank all his blood. She took him inside her body. He melted into her as an ice cube on a frying pan. When she finished dancing, she sat on the rock decorating her hair with shoe flowers and basil leaves. He will never part from her—body and soul. The unused bed of jasmine waited for a more suitable lover. The lover will not come until the end of the world when all the lustful men on earth have passed away.'

The elderly woman said no other word and left the room. The small golden cross that the woman was wearing made Fernandez remember his mother. 'Even the Christians over here believe in all these legends. It is going to very difficult to civilise India.' he thought. He entered the forest.

Fernandez enjoyed the beauty of the forest even though it was getting dark. The cool breeze made his mind calm. He could get the smell of the Pala flowers. He could hear the sound of the anklet. If another person entered the forest, he or she would be screaming with fear by now. Fernandez sat on a rock and watched the stream flowing. He took out a frog from the stream and held it in his hand. He started thinking. 'Fear can kill. Samuel would have died due to fear. The sound of this rare variety of frog resembles the sound of an anklet. He would have run in panic and would have been a victim of these slippery rocks.'

When Fernandez explored the forest, he found many traps nature had created. There were steep slopes that ended near cliffs. There were muddy ponds that could become a death trap. The presence of wild animals like leopards in the forest also helped Fernandez to solve an age-old mystery. He smiled to himself as if he knew everything on earth. All of a sudden, Fernandez was reminded of his mother. His mother was deeply worried because her son was an atheist. She said a rosary everyday for her son. Fernandez always spent time arguing with his mother about the lack of proof for the existence of God. She was never satisfied. She wanted her son to pray along with her but her son would always refuse. 'Truth,' she would say, 'can not be understood with human logic. It lies deep inside faith and love. It is something from the wisdom which was preserved through ages.'

When she died of small pox, Fernandez felt guilty for making his mother feel sad in the final days of her life. He wished that he had acted before his mother as a believer.

The villagers were surprised to see Fernandez in the morning. In the presence of the temple priest, he addressed the villagers, 'It is true. I saw the Yakshi. She did not kill me because she wanted to warn the people through me. She told me to warn the British government against the destruction of forestland to build the railways. She told me to warn husbands who drink and beat their wives . . .'

After Fernandez told everything he wanted to say, he left the village as the Yakshi who was invisible to everyone smiled.

80

'What do you think of my story?' asked Dominic

'An erotic horror tale to attack atheists like me.'

'It is not like that. It is about human beliefs and myths.'

'The elderly lady is a better storyteller than you are. It would have been a good detective story of you had worked harder. What is your next story about?'

'About a boy called Dominic who fell in love with a girl called Manju.'

'What happens in the end?'

'Dominic says—I love you.'

'And Manju asks—Do you really love me or do you love the way I inspire you to write stories? Do you love me or do you love the pleasure you are going to experience when I eat you up like a Yakshi?'

'Dominic is speechless.'

'Manju says—I love you.'

Manju left before Dominic could reply.

81

Dominic visited Fr. Ben late in the evening. He made some lime tea for Dominic and himself. Fr. Ben took a sip of tea and said, 'The smell of lime is very sublime. God's creations are great. God never said "Let there be religions". It is our prejudices that have created them. When God created man, His own image sprang into life in the form of an earthly being. The human soul is God. In ancient times, women thought their husbands as Gods and worshiped them. The mother saw God in the baby and loved it. A human saw God in his enemy and loved him. A human saw God in the most unholy men and loved them. Love and God can never be separated. It is our greed, selfishness, pride, prejudice, superstition and stupid desires that keeps us away from knowing ourselves. We are Gods when we love.'

Dominic quickly replied, 'In ancient times women were treated as slaves by the patriarchal system. They were forced to do things. So do you think that you are God? I think that is pride.'

'My boy Dominic', said Fr. Ben calmly, 'Let not what I am stop me from attaining heaven. I do not identify myself as a Roman Catholic priest from a rich family and caste from India. I identify myself as a creation of God. Everything that is born of love is born of God. Man kills man. Religion kills religion. Nation kills nation. God cannot be killed. A religious man lost in rituals, prayers, donations, offerings, sacraments and self-glory is a useless man if he does not know love. Everything is one in love. There are only two possibilities—there is only one religion in the whole world or every person has his /her own religion. What the world thinks is not the truth. Religion is a poison and spirituality is its antidote. Do you get the idea? So face all those useless religious people with the face of love—might be with a smile. However, be careful, you will be beaten if you smile at a girl for a long time. O! Time for my hot water bath.'

Dominic thought why Fr. Ben talked in a very artificial manner even though his speech sounded so natural. He thought of the sermon about the importance of prayer given by Fr. Ben. 'We pray yet we do not pray. Prayer should not be a mechanical activity but an echo full of love from the soul.' Dominic wondered why he always talked about love. He recalled the adjectives other people use while talking about Fr. Ben— psycho, mystic, evangelist, stupid.

82

Dominic was admiring the prizes he had won. It was the most memorable day; he would never forget this day throughout his life. That is when he saw Nithin; he looked very upset. Dominic always compared Nithin with Justine because both of them were known to be very religious. It took him a long time to realise that Nithin was actually quite different from Justine.

Justine took religion as a ritual, but Nithin did not. Nithin's mother always forced him to perform rituals; he respected his mother for what she was. After his father's death, the society forced a heavy burden on his shoulders. He was held responsible for his sister's elopement with a boy of another caste. Even after the incident, he did not stop loving his sister unlike his mother who was quite orthodox in her beliefs. 'At least she was able to run away from the ignoble society.' he would always say. Though it was a well-known fact that Nithin had financial problems he was never seen stooping before anyone. Whenever he talked about his problems, he always added a pinch of humour and deviated from the topic.

Nithin did not have enough money to pay the examination fees. He felt like asking Dominic for help. It was the last date to pay. 'I will try and see.' said Dominic. Dominic was busy thinking about the times he was called Abdullah.

83

When Abdullah was five, he wondered why he did not have parents. Did he come out from the fire as in the story one of his friends told him? His uncle brought him up. Everything about his parents was a mystery. He and his uncle were the only Muslims in their village near Rajasthan. Everybody respected them since they respected the Mughal rule. They were also known for their sense of discipline. Abdullah tried to be a true Muslim just like his uncle. The Divine One who is so merciful and forgiving fascinated him.

When Abdullah was fourteen, he saw a young girl being beaten by her young husband because she did not prepare good food. Abdullah felt sorry for her. She screamed with terror and looked into the darkness of the night. She saw Abdullah's kind eyes behind a tiny lamp.

'What are you looking at?' asked the young husband.

'Just heard some noise and got curious.'

84

The young husband's name was Prithviraj. He used to often chat and play with Abdullah. 'Wives these days do not make good food. My mother was right.' he said. Abdullah soon changed the topic.

Abdullah was a person who hated violence. May be it was because of his aversion for blood. When he saw farmers beating their cows he felt like crying. The cow for him was not a holy animal or the symbol of motherhood but a creation of God that has the right to live happily. He felt the others would find his feeling very childish. Therefore, he did not express his feelings to anyone.

84

His uncle got Abdullah married to a thirteen-year-old blind girl because he did not have enough money to spend as dowry. 'God has asked us to serve the poor. By marrying a poor blind girl God will see you as his faithful servant and honour you in paradise.' said his uncle. He found the girl for Abdullah from a far away village that had many Muslims. Abdullah wondered why his uncle loved to live a lonely life. Was he a fakir?

Hasseena, the girl Abdullah married shivered as he came close to her. Abdullah asked so many questions about her village. His kind voice disrobed all her fears. 'My mother talked a lot about the cruelty of husbands and about the pain of giving birth to young babies.'

Hasseena had a black mole on her face that prevented her from getting a husband for a long time.

'Do I look ugly' she asked touching her black mole. Abdullah replied, 'You are the most beautiful girl I have ever seen. Everybody notices only your black mole but I see your white body, your chubby cheeks, your softness, your curvy breasts, your thin legs, your pretty hips and your . . . ' and Abdullah gave a soft kiss on her lips.

Abdullah was scared to make love to Hasseena because she was very weak and sensitive. He would hug her and plant kissed on her face. He felt very great when they held hands. She found it lovely to put her hands over his shoulders and go for a walk.

85

Prithviraj's wife, Rukmani always used to talk with Hasseena when Abdullah goes to work. Sometimes Rukmani took her to her house and prepared lunch for her. Prithviraj did not like this. According to him, a blind girl brought ill luck to the house she entered.

Once Hasseena asked Abdullah, 'Why don't you make love to me?'

'Will you feel pain if I made love to you?' asked Abdullah.

'I don't mind if I die making love to you. I am always ready to please you. Will you please me?'

'Yes, I will.'

There was some sound outside. They heard someone coming. When Abdullah opened the door, he found Prithviraj standing there with his friends.

'Will you come with us tonight?' he asked.

Abdullah whispered in Hasseena's ear, 'I will come tomorrow and make love to you.' before leaving the house.

86

When Abdullah along with Prithviraj's gang were nearing a forest Abdullah asked, 'Why are we going to the forest? I thought we are going to have our usual conference.'

'We are going to enjoy the liquor and women that are waiting for us. This is going to be our best night.'

'I will not come. This is against my beliefs. I do not want to be part of this sin. I am going back.'

Prithviraj and his friends called him a coward and tried their best but Abdullah was strong in his beliefs. They cursed Abdullah and went forward.

When Abdullah reached home, it was midnight. Abdullah decided to surprise Hasseena by giving her the greatest pleasure she would experience in her entire life. Abdulla felt Hasseena sleeping in the corner. His hand groped like a wild scorpion over her body. He felt her softness with gentle pinches. She sighed. He cuddled with her and felt her warmth. His passion conquered himself. He gave away himself to her. Hasseena started teasing him with licks and bites. He moulded her like clay and discovered greater pleasures. After nibbling her ears he whispered, 'Sleep well during daytime.' He wiped his sweat with her lustrous hair and did not let her sleep that night.

When morning brought in light, Abdulla looked at Hasseena's face.

'Rukmani, is it you?' said a shocked Abdulla, 'Don't tell anyone. Where is Hasseena?'

Hasseena was sleeping in the other end of the room not knowing what had happened.

'I am a great sinner. I have committed adultery. I am going to hell.' thought a guilty Abdulla. That night Abdulla tried his best while making love to Hasseena to give her heart delights. Hasseena moved from one realm of ecstasy to another. 'I can see all the love in this world which God has given me though I can't see.' she said without seeing the guilty scorn on Abdulla's face.

87

Every time Abdulla was home his hands groped like a five headed snake over Hasseena's body as if he was trying to make up for the sin he had committed. The bites of his nails were lovely. As a young python trying to swallow an egg, he used to put Hasseena's bosom into his mouth. The python of his conscience started to swallow his mind. Hasseena felt as if Abdulla was part of her body. When Abdulla looked at Hasseena's face Rukmani's face came into his mind. *Did they look similar?* Abdulla cursed his gift of sight. Another sin.

Snakes are beautiful but poisonous. Some say they use their poison for self-defence. However, that is not true. They use their poison to paralyse their victims. Cobras make love for hours. They also build beautiful nests to protect the eggs. However, many other snakes leave their eggs to fate. There is something mysterious about snakes. *Are they Gods? Are the demons?*

89

Abdulla went to see a fakir. To him Abdulla asked a question which he feared to ask his uncle, 'If a man commits adultery will God forgive him?'

'God is all forgiving,' said the respectable man, 'Good deeds can wash away the sins of the past.'

'What are good deeds?' asked Abdulla.

'True and honest worship to the Most Merciful Master of the Day of Judgement. Love and sacrifice for the betterment of humanity. Son, why do you ask such questions?'

'My soul needed answers.'

'You have won great graces from God for being his kind servant and choosing to marry a poor woman when you could have got a rich woman.'

Abdulla was surprised that the Fakir knew a lot about him.

'Beware!' warned the Fakir, 'Eblis is trying his best to lead you into temptations.'

90

A common man said, 'Shah Jahan, our emperor, is the greatest lover. No one on earth can make love as Shah Jahan. It is a pity;his dearest wife passed away. He is going to build a giant monument for her.'

A poet came forward and sang a few songs about the love of Shah Jahan. Another poet came and sang a song about the beauty of Mumtaz. He compared the timeless beauty of Mumtaz to the timeless beauty of the moon. He had tears in his eyes.

'My love is nothing compared to the love Shah Jahan had for his wife Mumtaz', thought Abdulla.

91

When Abdulla went home everyone around him looked silent except for his uncle who said,'Hasseena died after giving birth to a stillborn baby. She died on the same day Emperess Mumtaz left this world.'

'I am responsible for this', thought Abdulla as tears blinded his eyes, 'I spilled poison into her. My sin has made my love juice poisonous.'

Later that day after a small talk with Pritiviraj Abdulla saw Rukmani with a baby. When no one was looking, she whispered into Abdulla's ears, 'You have given me a son.'

92

'From henceforth, you will have to pay heavy taxes to build the Taj Mahal. We will select men from your village. They will have to help in bringing marble stones from Rajasthan to Agra. No money will be given. Enough food will be given. You will be rewarded after the work is done.' said the royal messenger.

Both Pritiviraj and Abdulla would have to leave the village in a week. Pritiviraj whipped Rukmani.

93

'I will not work. I am not coming. The Emperor of yours is cheating us all. He is robbing the dignity of our wives to glorify the dignity of his. He is stealing from the masses to satisfy his sexual fantasy. Do you know how many people are going to die of starvation because of the Emperor's vanity?' said Pritiviraj to a soldier who was busy trying to get more and more people for labour. Abdulla licked Rukmani's wound marks that the whip gave her. Rukmani had wound marks on her thighs, breasts, hands, hips, belly and shoulders. Pritiviraj shouted at the soldier who shouted back. The soldier started beating Pritiviraj all over his body. His body began to shiver with a biting pain. Rukmani hummed with pleasure and pain when her wounds were being healed. Abdulla rubbed a thick sticky medicine on her wounds using an oiling cloth. The soldier kicked Pritiviraj on his groin. His mind went blank. His heart started to beat faster. He opened his mouth as if trying to vomit out the pain. Abdulla dipped his legs into a pot of cold medicinal oil and massaged her body. His toe moved in circles and closed all her wounds. When her body was fully oiled, she looked like a golden sculpture. Her shiny body was a treat to Abdulla's eyes. Rukmani got up and touched his frame with her body. The oil and medicine acted as a gum and stuck the two bodies together. His chest expanded with masculinity. Her breasts, like two thirsty does, drank the waters of his maleness. She massaged Abdulla's thighs with her soft legs. Abdulla's groin felt its softness. Rukmani used her natural wound as an oiling cloth and rubbed the length and breadth of Abdulla's legs with it. The oiling cloth oiled Abdulla's hands, belly, chest and face. When the oiling cloth touched the heart of Abdulla's forehead, he felt as if a divine radiance overflowed from his mind. The soldier kicked on Pritiviraj's chest. Pritiviraj hit the soldier on his head. The soldier began to bleed. He started shouting, 'My mind is breaking into pieces.' Abdulla massaged Rukmani's hair with perfume while she blessed his lips with soft kisses. Rukmani used her tongue and lips to make each kiss more passionate than the previous one. The heat waves that she poured into Abdulla's lips were too much for him. He had to stop this. He bit Rukmani's lower lips so hard that it began to bleed. The pleasure diluted the pain. Blood is always tasty. They drank it. Pritiviraj enjoyed the stream of blood that flowed from the soldier's head like how a child would enjoy a waterfall. He laughed with vengeance. Abdulla poured water over Rukmani and started bathing her like a nurse who bathes a newborn baby. His kissed her passionately and let his tongue explore into her depths. His lips sailed over her body with his tongue as a sail, moving along with the tides and braving her tempestuous heat it sank into her groin. When Rukmani almost fainted with love, Abdulla playfully tickled her body. Her bottom was the most ticklish part of her body. She moved her hands and legs like a newborn baby. Abdulla caught her neck and looked into her face. Her hands and legs stopped moving. Her lips began to shiver. Another soldier came from nowhere and caught hold of Pritiviraj's neck. He in turn caught the soldier's neck and looked into his face. The face of the soldier resembled Shah Jahan. Rukmani's face resembled Hasseena. Pritiviraj screamed with anger. Rukmani's infant began to cry. The soldier uttered a war cry. The baby boy sucked milk from Rukmani's right breast while Abdulla sucked her left bosom; Abdulla used his lips, tongue and saliva with a terrible vigour that the baby was ignorant about. The baby's hand was not long enough to express love and conquer over Rukmani's femininity and torture it with stabbings but Abdullah's hand was. Many soldiers surrounded Pritiviraj. Abdullah's rough hand dived into the deepest parts of Rukmani's love wound. His fingers were long and hairy. He rotated his fingers in all directions. Her love wound savoured his fingers with a good appetite. She remained motionless that the infant who was now sleeping will not be disturbed. She gently carried the baby and left it in the next room. One of the soldiers poked a small knife into Pritiviraj's stomach. He could not move. Rukmani closed her eyes as if waiting for an arrow to strike her anytime. Abdulla surrendered his organ into her. She moved her hips from side to side to give the organ joy. When Pritiviraj screamed, he thought of his wife and son. *I should have kissed them both before he went. I should have not whipped my wife.* The soldier was bloodthirsty. The knife went into Pritiviraj's body repeatedly. Pain waves from his stomach darted into his brain. Abdulla's organ darted into Rukmani repeatedly. When the organ could not hold on any longer Abdulla's life fluid flowed into her. Abdulla did not find a better place to throw his melancholy into. Pritiviraj knew that he was dying. He wanted to throw all his sadness, anger and revenge somewhere. He wanted to die like a hero. *Rukmani is smiling at me. The wind is gentle. Rukmani says, 'My hero!'* As he was about to fall Pritiviraj picked up a stone and hit the cruel soldier with it crying, 'Let us die together'. Rukmani cried, 'Let us die together, my hero!' 'So shall we.' replied Abdulla. They fell down dead. They fell down as if they were dead.

Death silences all words, passions and senses. The body has finished its work and worth. Death is not an end it is just the beginning. The dead lose something to gain something even greater. We go back into nature and become dust, soil, humus, leaves and flowers. We blow out the lamp that our birth lit. We make space for the younger generation. We set our soul free from the cage of our body. We are no longer mortals. We are immortals from then on. We all die.

94

The sad news of his friend's death reached Abdulla. He imagined how Pritiviraj might have fallen dead. The imagination was designed by the emotion of guilt. He cried.

The sad news of her husband's death reached Rukmani. She imagined how he might have fallen dead. Her imagination was blocked by the image of Abdulla and the emotion of passionate love. She touched her vulva and felt its hunger and thirst. *He must go to help Shah Jahan make love to his dead wife. He must leave.* She cried.

95

Abdulla watched a train of elephants pulling marble blocks to Agra. An elephant rider fainted. 'You should replace him', said a soldier to Abdulla.

'I do not know how to control an elephant', he replied.

'Then learn.'

Abdullah could not say 'no' to the soldier's advice.

Heavy work after heavy work was loaded over Abdulla giving him no time to think. Once when the night was chill Abdulla thought, 'Love does not exist on this earth. What exists is obsession which drives people mad.'

Abdulla thought about his own obsession and the new sin he had committed by blaspheming love. He remembered about what his teachers taught him about God and love. Abdulla decided not to think evil about love again. Abdulla decided not to feel guilty again.

96

The heat from the white marble burned Abdulla's barefoot. The stones he carried wearied his muscles. His facial beauty and virility had faded away. He was a slave, an animal caged for eternity, struggling hopelessly. On his back lay the whips of the master. In the face of the master, he saw the fear for a higher master.

Between the dust and heat, he heard the voice of an old man. Abdulla bravely put down his stone and followed the voice.

It was more than a voice. It was a cry. The old man was crying for water. The old man's face looked like a dry leaf. One of his eye sockets was hollow. His ears were torn. A hole in his cheek showed his only surviving tooth. Abdulla took some cold water and quenched his thirst. The old man's only eye looked into Abdulla's eyes and said, 'Thank you!' Abdulla's heart shivered. He went back and carried his stone before the master could catch him idling about.

That night he discovered that his heart was empty. All the sins of his life had been washed away. Was it the realisation of the joy of giving? Was it a newfound love for humanity? Was it the soul winning over the body? Even Abdulla could not guess. Abdulla remembered the lines from the scriptures that talked about charity. *Allah knows all. He sees me. He designed the world and its beauties to teach something more valuable in life. Subhanallah!*

97

The greatest joy comes from love—the love that possessed Abdulla's soul when he forgot his own existence and helped the poor workers to let them enjoy bits and pieces of happiness among the weary struggle of life. Many workers would have felt that life is meaningless if not for Abdulla who quietly reminded them of the dew in the desert. Abdulla was scarcely fed. Masters often threatened him with death. However, Abdulla had conquered death with love.

98

It took twenty-two years to build the Taj Mahal—twenty-two years of torture, twenty-two years of royal ego. The architect of the Taj Mahal was lying amongst stones with his hands cut-off by the emperor who did not want the world to build another Taj Mahal. He remembered the gifts he had received, the comforts he had enjoyed, the beautiful women he touched and the face of the Queen before she died. He was the only other person except for the emperor who had ever made love to Queen Mumtaz. The Emperor had force him to do it. He believed that it would give him the inspiration to build the greatest monument on earth. He watched the Emperor dipping his organ into the blood of a goat. He had watched the Emperor raping the Queen many times. The Emperor wanted to have a hundred children with her. She looked more fertile and gorgeous than any woman on earth did. She had large eyes, large breasts and magnificent hips yet she could not have more than fourteen. The third wife of Shah Jahan was human after all. Was he? The architect was trying his best to cry, but he could not. Abdulla went near him and fed him with a few apples. 'Do not feed me.', said the architect, 'You remember! It was I who ordered fifty whips for you.'

'Love has no memory.' replied Abdulla.

99

After a gap of twenty-two years, Abdulla visited his good old village. His village had changed a lot. There were big buildings all around. Only a few huts were seen. A small crowd came crying. They were carrying the body of a dead girl to be cremated. Abdulla saw a few people dressed in rags eating greedily by the roadside. His deserted house was completely refashioned to look like a military base. Rukmani's house was intact.

Abdulla saw his son and Rukmani. Both looked as if they had only skin and bones in their bodies. The ugliness of human vanity and greed were drawn on their bodies. The poverty had done this. The tax had done this. The Taj Mahal had done this. When someone or something is forced to look more beautiful, someone or something is forced to look uglier.

Abdulla's son wanted to speak something to his father but he could not. Rukmani struggled a lot to utter, 'We are dying'. Abdulla brought food and water for them. But this could not stop Abdulla from seeing the death of his own son. *Why had he waited so long to die?* Rukmani did not cry. Abdulla knew why.

From that moment, Abdulla decided to do everything to save his village.

100

Abdulla spent all his money to help the people around him. Abdulla realised that this was the way God wanted him to wash away sins. Abdulla brought milk, grains and fruits for the starving multitudes. He bought rags to protect their naked bodies from the cold. He made small carts when he had nothing else to do. He befriended the soldiers with his work and got money to help the suffering village. 'A day will come when you should eat everything you have and prepare for an exodus.' Abdulla always reminded them. He experienced the greatest of pleasures when he poured water into thirsty mouths. When Abdulla found that all doors were closed before him he realised that the only way he could save his villagers was to break open the door of the great barn where all the grains and vegetables stayed hidden to satisfy the royal gluttons.

That night Abdulla decided to steal the royal barn that was filled with the fruits of the sweat of the poor villagers. Abdulla joined all the small carts he had gifted to the soldiers and filled them with the grains and vegetables that he had daringly stolen from the barn. He walked slowly into the street and distributed them secretly to the hungry villagers who already knew about the plan. Abdulla also found a lot of money hidden in the barn. He distributed it equally among the villagers.

Abdulla who wanted everything to look like an accident set the empty barn on fire. He did not notice the soldiers on night patrol who caught him doing this act. The soldiers surrounded him. 'I am a mad man.', cried Abdulla, 'I burned down all your food. I love burning food.'

'Kill the mad man!' cried one of the soldiers.

Abdulla ran into the barn. The soldiers followed him. Fire fell over them.

101

When Abdulla gained consciousness, he knew that the burns on his body were deep. He was the reason for the death of a few soldiers. His hands were tied up and the soldiers who were around him were cursing him with harsh words. A huge group of soldiers who came to the village for collecting taxes were also present. They were surprised to find the village empty. The villagers had left for time being with their fortune.

'We all know that you have done this. We will find your people and kill them one by one. Tonight we are going to kill you in a very cruel manner.' said the commander of soldiers with a wicked smile on his face.

That night when it was time to perform the cruel act the soldiers heard a strange music. The sand was rolling in the air. The ghosts of Hasseena and Rukmani arose from the sand. They look surprisingly young and healthy. Their eyes were burning with orange flames. Their souls were visible bouncing from their head to toe. They held hands and smiled at each other. When the soldiers saw them, they were stunned. They were in pain. All of them felt the blood that leaked from their ears and nose. They all fell down dead.

The ghosts came close to Abdulla and kissed him on his cheek. He forgot all his pains. He felt a strange kind of ecstasy. He watched the soul of Hasseena merging with the soul of Rukmani. They flew into the heavens as a single being.

A few minutes later Abdulla died a joyful death.

102

Dominic told Manju,'I love you, but it is not the so-called romantic love. I love you as a good human being. I love talking with you. I love being your friend. I have my own identity. I have my own dreams. I do not know whether I have hurt you anyway. Your beauty infatuated me. It was just my stupid feelings that I have no control over. I . . .'

Manju laughed and then gave a small smile and said, 'Hmm . . . Have any questions, friend?'

'What are you going to do after the exams?'

'Going to tour the world! Seriously, I signed for a package.'

Manju looked very happy.

'Joy is the aim of love.' thought Dominic, 'If Manju remains happy beyond the world of my love I will be happy too. I do not have to possess her to love her. The end of love need not be romance. If you are prepared to fall in love, you should also be prepared to fall out of it. Love is not an excuse to get married.'

'Why are you smiling?' asked Manju.

'Thinking about what I am going to do after I finish my MA.'

103

ACT FOUR

Chorus:

The rivals wanted to take a break.

Therefore, they do not break each other.

They decided to play a tricky game.

The name of the game to tame each other

Was called 'I agree'.

[The Novelist was teaching Dominic to make a cake. The Novelist decided to talk to Dominic.]

Novelist: You may criticise me for many things but I am being truthful and sincere. I have included excerpts from your autobiography to bring out your point of view. I have included our arguments in the novel so that the readers may not be carried away by fiction.

Dominic: I agree with you. May be my story needs to be told. Maybe you are right. I never wanted to publish my autobiography. It is meant to be a secret. My true story must not be mixed with sex and fantasy. I hate to read such things. You are a sadist.

Novelist: I agree. I have written filthy words. I have celebrated immorality, but separating sex from literature is like separating the body from the soul. Sex in excess with make one an animal but totally avoiding it will make one a soulless stone. God's greatest gift must not be forsaken.

Sexuality is the relationship between the body and the mind and spirituality is the relationship between the mind and the body; it cannot be separated. Why should certain human experiences be hidden from words? Have you unconsciously felt them, played with them and loved them? Sex is sometimes love, sometimes lust and sometimes passion. The stories of Padmini, Immanuel and Abdulla represent love, lust and passion respectively.

Dominic: I agree. I understand. I love the Shah Jahan of the history textbooks. You have made him the villain of your novel. You have killed culture and tradition. You are a big liar.

Novelist: I agree. The villain is nothing but the image the hero sees in his mirror.

Dominic: I agree. Is your novel a tribute to short stories or is it a psychological study on what happens to the mind of a male post-teenage? Is it a combination of all filthy tricks to get a reader to read a book? There is no sense or meaning inside your novel.

Novelist: I agree. It is a novel. Let sense and meaning stay outside my novel. Let them keep knocking forever at the gates of my novel. I will not open. I will just shout at them, 'Those fools outside my novel need you more'. My talent is to write and I need to write. I have the instinct of a writer. I live to write.

Dominic: Ok . . . ok.

[The Novelist rubs the cream of the cake on Dominic's face.]

Novelist: Say, I agree!

104 (a)

Dominic still remembered each and every incident that happened in his past three lives. His brain bounced with thoughts about them. He saw Nithin walking towards him from a distance. Dominic unconsciously put his hand in his pocket. He felt a thousand rupee note. 'My God!' he thought, 'I did not lose the thousand-rupee note. I put it into my pocket instead of putting it into my purse.'

Dominic gave the money to Nithin. Dominic saw the happiness on Nithin's face. He smiled gently. His smile resembled the smile of an omniscient Hindu god. Dominic remembered a joke Nithin had told him months ago, 'When I looked at my dying father I was abhorred by his ugly looking skinny face. Then I remembered something that I had read in a book that said that human could be freed from all bondages and achieve heaven only if they see God in the faces of all human beings. My Dad, then, looked like a lucky guy who got a second chance to be innocent like baby Jesus. He died after a few minutes and I smiled when I saw a halo around his head. My Mom was wailing her heart out; I think she did not see the halo. She, of course, was another image of God. God litters His images in mysterious ways . . .'

The joke was interrupted by my recollection of a fragment from the famous prayer by St.Francis of Assissi that was often misused and manipulated throughout the academic year, 'To give is to receive . . .'

104 (b)

Dominic looked at the grass moving to the tunes of the breeze and felt like a yellow butterfly that moved crookedly through the green spikes of grass romancing the tiny purple flowers; it was a feeling of weightlessness. The sky grew darker and everything turned into shadows; the crows sang in chorus as background music to the game of shadows.

Dominic entered into his room and smiled at Justine and Shabri; they smiled back.

'Few more days!' exclaimed Shabri. He had changed a lot from the revolutionary youngster he once was. He had learned to move like grass when the wind blows. His bed was piled up with books on philosophy and spirituality including the Holy Bible, the Imitations of Christ, the Bagavat Gita, the Holy Koran and a book on Sufi mysticism. Keeping his bed untidy was part of his nature; a cosmic ocean of divine wisdom occupied his place of slumber. He had dived into the ocean of spirituality and had reached depths that Justine had never dreamt about.

'For the past two hours there is no power,' said Justine squashing a mosquito, 'they say that the current will come only at 2:00 am.' Dominic nodded.

They walked to the mess together talking about mosquito problems and retuned talking about insomnia.

When they returned, Dominic curled up in bed to sleep while Justine and Shabri kept on talking. Dominic's attempt to sleep was foiled by the heat and the excitement that was running inside his head. He listened to the conversation.

'Justine, I loved the Imitations of Christ.' said Shabri, 'It is one of the books that have changed my way of thinking.'

'Yes, it is a great book.' replied Justine.

A few moments passed without any conversation.

'What were you thinking about?' asked Shabri.

'About Sr. Monica.' said Justine in a dreamy voice.

'Of late, you have become very friendly with her. Has she become your spiritual mentor?'

'Yes, May be. She has changed my life. She has taught me something that I have never dared to learn.'

'Can you share it with me? Did God appear before you or her?'

'No, but He did deep inside my soul. Can you promise me that you will not tell this to anyone?'

'Sure.'

'As you have always said Sr. Monica was the island of the class.' Began Justine softly, 'She was the only one who did not jump and shout when the college band performed. She never bunked class nor did she visit exotic restaurants. She preferred silence to chaos. No one had the time to contemplate about her beauty, but I did. She was the one who introduced me to books like the Imitations of Christ and the Bagavat Gita and I introduced them to you. We read and discussed together, her and me. I told her that if she were not a nun I would have made her my girlfriend. I taught her to be more active in the college and she taught me to be more active spiritually. My idea about God was very orthodox and mundane. I never talked to God as a friend, but she made me to do it. I saw her as an angel send by God and sometimes thought that she was God. A month back, we got close to each other as never before. As you already know, we were the main volunteers at the Gabriel religious convention. On one of those nights, when the convention was still going on, we found ourselves alone in an old sports shed that is now used for dumping old stage items. A 240v yellow bulb lit the room. As Sr. Monica was cleaning the room with a broom, she jarred the door. I went close to her and kissed her forehead. Our eyes moved closer. I expected her to protest, but she came forward and kissed my lips. How soft was it! How divine is a holy kiss! The kiss caressed the interiors of my soul. We loosened our clothes and they obeyed the laws of gravity. The black scapular that she wore graced her neck and prompted me to kiss her nape and the curvaceous line that her spine had drawn. She kissed me with a passion I had not known for years. When did I feel it before? It was when, as a thirteen year old, I played doctor—patient with my female cousin, curing her stomach pain. It was when, as a fourteen year old, I undressed my sister's Barbie doll. She touched my body, healed my hammering heart, and lit the lamp of love that had remained unlit for years. I touched her as I would touch a heavenly idol left in the sanctum and glorified the creation of God. What miracle had God stored in the kissable mouths of women? I kissed her lips with a holy fire burning in my heart and heard the song 'Hallelujah!' being performed in the convention hall. Was the kiss similar to the kiss Isaac planted on the lips of Rebecca? Was the kiss sweeter than wine?

Another Songs of Solomon must be written to describe it. When the song stopped, we took back our lips and hugged each other. 'God has asked us to love one another.' she whispered in my ears. 'You are God's greatest creation.' I whispered in her ears. 'You and I are just small grains in the ocean of God's marvelous creation.' she whispered back. We fell in love. It was not lust, attachment or passion; it was pure love.'

'Justine!' exclaimed Shabri, 'You are a poet. You have changed a lot.'

'We may not meet again but the lamp of love has ignited in my soul. It is love.' said Justine and returned into silence. Passion can make a monk write erotic songs; intelligence would just swoon and fall at its feet.

104 (c)

Dominic's mind was excited with thoughts that it obstructed sleep. He thought, 'Where my previous births hallucinations? Would I have taken the same decisions if I did not remember my past three births? I could have enjoyed my college life with girlfriends and entertainments with a large space in my mind for short-term pleasures. [Novelist's observation: Men always see women as temptations in order to hide their sin and guilt] I could have got addicted to porn and drugs like Shabri; I could have tasted cigarette and liquor like him. I am glad he has changed. I could have done a lot of things, but I am glad I did not. It is not my previous births that have stopped me from doing things, but my native place, my culture, my environment, my grandmother's care, my spiritual scruples, my books, my life experiences and my precious soul that has touched me with a magical wand. Self-restraint is the force that resurrects humans from the slimy traps of nature. It is self-control and faith that can create a world, built with the bricks of love and peace, were all living beings live in harmony. Heaven will not be distant dream anymore. Thy kingdom come on earth as it is in heaven.'

Dominic fell asleep.

When he left Chennai and returned to his native place, he forgot about his previous births and was lost in the beauty of life.

I would like to end my novel like this, but the truth has some more things to say. I hate happy endings; it makes you feel that you are the only one living a unhappy life.

105

A young man decided that he should realise the infinity as soon as possible. He wanted to see the face of God and fill the bag of his mind with the breeze of infinite love. The things of the world were of no interest to him. He knew how vain they were. He decided to go on a long pilgrimage in search of God and Love.

'Where are you going?' asked his mother, 'Come and taste the chocolate cake I made for you.'

'No, I will not.' replied the son, 'I am going to attain spiritual realization.'

'Where are you going?' asked his girlfriend, 'Can we take a walk in the woods?'

'No, I will not.' replied the boyfriend, 'I do not care about the physical love that you can offer.'

The young man searched and searched but could not find God and Love throughout his life.

—The Novelist

01/01/2012

106

[Continued from 76]I, Dominic tried to write an autobiography but then I realised that I have secrets to keep that I would not like to share. Anyway, I wrote it. It is more like a recollection of the past. Am I justified? Why am I afraid of people around me? What is making the fear? What is stopping me from going out of my room to see the world? How can I make this world a better place? Am I lazy or am I selfish? Do I lack self-confidence? What is the meaning of life? What is? I am not trying to be philosophical. I am just trying to find the answers to my problems. A book has been written on me that is going to be published. Will the description of incidents and experiences do any good to this autobiography? I cannot find the object that is stopping me from making my own choices. I went to do my degree. I fell in love with books. I was ill-treated by 'friends'. I felt lonely at times. I acted in plays. I always played small parts. I wrote plays that were never staged. I participated in competitions but never won prizes. I made a good friend who was interested in books and movies. I could not meet him often. I got my degree. Then I went to another college to do my masters. My parents say I am lazy. They did not accept my intention of becoming a writer or a movie-maker. They are only hobbies according to them. My sister says I am selfish. I think it is true. I always wanted to help other but ended up thinking about myself. I boasted that if I saw a man injured on the road I will take him to the hospital risking everything even if it is the day of the final examination. When I went out to but a pillow a middle aged man fell before me from the first floor from a building. There was no blood. I could not move my finger. People came running from a distance and took the man to the hospital. I walked forward to buy a pillow. I must learn to love. Kamasutra did not help me. I was once fascinated about that book. The third chapter of Kamasutra talked about women's education centuries before any European book could. But the rest of the book is trash. I found it sexist, patriarchal, racist and casteist. I guess it was written to control the spread of Buddhism. After reading Kamasutra read the Bramacharcharya chapter from M.K.Gandhi's My Experiments with Truth. That would be a good dessert. Assisi College was quite good. Tying a degree on a string and making donkeys run after it was a good motivational idea. It is better than sitting simply at home wondering what to do next. Deadlines, fears and exams keep us all busy forgetting to get to ourselves. Believe me, no course teaches us to control our minds. Why don't we give everything we have to the poor? Why do we love to make money? Why do we think sex is everything? It is because our minds are selfish. Can prayer solve this? I have not tried it. I must try. I hate all those commercial ego-centred Indian films that say that unless you box up twenty martial arts experts and marry the most beautiful woman around you are a fool. We are all fools. Heroes are caught up between the reels. We can't fully blame films for making us over-ambitious. They just mirror the society. I don't have a girlfriend. Maybe because other young men are putting 'Fair and Handsome' to improve their 'Axe effect'. Maybe there is a girl who does not put 'Fair and Lovely' with a lot of pimples waiting for me. Beauty is only mind deep. Beauty is illusion at its best. Hear! O great minds fed with Coco-Cola and Lays chips. Human instinct—wah! I know that a child with a school will dream of getting good marks. When he gets good marks he would aspire of going to a good college. When he gets there he would fancy walking with a girlfriend besides him. I know that she will never be his. After college he would wish for a job and when he gets it he must be in need of a wife. After marriage, he dreams of children and having them makes them to undergo all the tortures that he had undergone when he was a child. They also get married. I know that he will then dream of retiring. He will get sick, roll with pain and wish for death. Death will satisfy his dreams and walk as a girlfriend beside him until they are finally united. I know about the religions and the philosophies of the world, yet when I am dead hungry I would steal food for survival just as an uneducated person does. I know all this stuff, yet as I am writing these lines I fancy walking with a girlfriend besides me and I know she does not exist. In Assisi College I met Fr.Ben who changed the way I think. I met Raguvaran's friend of Fr.Ben who was quite interested in my behaviour. He called himself a yogi. He believed that the greatest asana was to dance without control in a club with the members of the opposite sex forgetting about your own gender. Dance is the greatest meditation which will ultimately result in self-realisation and nirvana. He loved nude paintings of both men and women. He deeply admired the nude paintings of Ingres and at the same time was fascinated by the mural paintings of Kerala and the Khajuraho sculptures. He was immersed in painting Krishna and his gopis. When M F Hussain's painting of Mother India in the nude was talked about he would say, 'Those who draw Mother India clad in a sari are scoundrels and hypocrites. They try to stereotype her with a few elitist Indian women who can afford a shining sari. Her nakedness symbolises her peace, truth and non-violence. Her nudity symbolises her universality, her beauty and her closeness with nature.' He told me that he would share a secret with me. It is a mantra that makes you remember the things that happen in your past three births. I did not believe him in the beginning. One day on a sunny morning I saw him sitting by the roadside buying used novels. I sat opposite to him. He looked into my eyes for a while. He gave me a piece of paper with the mantra written in Sanskrit. Sanskrit was my second language at school. The mantra echoed into my soul. I was reborn. I did not remember my past three births as the novelist claims. It said, 'The Divine Soul, the Kingdom of Heaven, the Supreme Soul is within You; escape from your body using the Love and Peace as wings into it and bathe in its oceans of bliss.' I don't know what the novelist understands. I do not believe in reincarnation. It can be used as a literary device, but not like the way the novelist has used it. My life is an open book. It will go on. The novelist has promised me half of the royalty. That is good of him, but he cannot rewrite my life; it is I who has lived it. An autobiography should never end. The journey will continue. The journey of a soul will never end. [To be continued]

107

Nathi, the princess of Balapur, was travelling through a forest to see King Artha who dreamed of marrying her. She was wearing the beautiful silk garment that was presented to her by Artha. On the way she saw a naked nun meditating in the forest. She looked young and beautiful. The men around her were singing praises. 'Who is that?' the princess asked to her charioteer. 'That is Jalam, the great goddess of nature who protects the forest', he replied.

'I know you are not a goddess.' Nathi shouted her, 'Why are you not wearing any clothes? Are you not ashamed? You are questioning the dignity of women. You are a whore.'

Jalam asked, 'How many silk worms did they kill to make that garment?'

Nathi was silent. She came out from the cocoon of her garments and meditated near Jalam. Nathi was never again polluted by clothes and wore only the skin that God and Nature had presented her. There were no artificial barriers to separate her from God and Nature. She never again thought of exploiting Nature to manufacture clothes.

Jalam turned into a spirit and entered into the silk garment. Numerous silkworms emerged from the garment which was not seen anymore. Jalam like a glow-worm flew into the heavens.

'God has created us naked.

Why should we meddle with God's creation?

God has made us beautiful.

Why should we hide our beauty?' sang the devotees.

Nathi became the great goddess of Nature.

—The Novelist

30/01/2012

108

'You say people don't talk with you', argued the psychologist, 'But do you talk to people?'

'No, something is stopping me.', replied Dominic, 'I wish I had got more marks. I wish I had travelled around the world. I wish I had known how to drive. I wish I had gone for more movies without my parents. I wish I had travelled without the fear of being lonely.'

'What do you do to make yourself happy?'

'I read books. I watch movies. I like to do them when I am alone. I fear people, especially strangers. I spend time in imagination and masturbation. I think both of them are the same. I told you about planet Zod. I also had my Kingdom Runa where the king used to expand his empire by marrying princesses. I was also the tribal chief Mora who made love with young women as a ritual before they got married.'

'These are the works of the unconscious mind. In real life, we do not do such things or our culture does not permit us to do it. You might have heard about the super-ego. Now look at this picture. What is it?'

'An oasis?'

'Yes, now make a story out of it.'

'I was living in an oasis surrounded by far-reaching deserts. I was alone. God gave me a gift of giving lives to the sand sculptures I made. I made beautiful female forms with voluptuous bodies with sand and water. Their brains were not mature enough to think independently. They just obeyed my commands like animals. I gave life to a tiger with the wings of an eagle as a security. The biggest flaw of my creation was that the life

I poured into them lasted only for a year. I had to bury them up and create new maidens. I was selfish and did not give enough food for a few maidens and they died of hunger. I did not have food for all. I decided to make only a single maiden for the next years. However, a single maiden made me bored. I made women with different features. I made one without hands and legs. I made one with giant breasts and hips, one as a dwarf, one with long hands and legs, one with big eyes, one with a long neck, one with six breasts, one with ten vaginas in different parts of her body, one with an enlarged clitoris and many more. I made love with all of them and got different types of pleasures. Still I was angry and lonely. I made a slave with his penis in the place of his nose and his nose in the place of his penis. I called him Nose. He was my favorite slave. Once when I got very angry I killed him. I killed others too for the shortage of food. God was very angry. He said, "I created you, Man, to protect this world and love others. Where are your human qualities? What are you after? Do you consider greed as the only virtue? You could not see others as one of your own kind. You did not notice that the short life span of your creations was a curse." I said, "They do not talk to me even though I try hard to teach them. I love them but they do not love me. They only obey my orders." God than replied, "Who asked you to command? You did not love them. You only loved the pleasure you got from them. If you had loved any of them, I would have shown you the road to paradise. Now you may go to hell." So saying God threw me to hell.'

'You are a good story teller. It also has a good message. I think you summarized the whole history of the human race in this story. Do you think your stories are a bit vulgar?'

'If the novelist can do it why can't I?'

'Why don't you write down your feelings and emotions? Do not hide anything in your mind; just write. Vulgar or not, do not repress anything in your mind. So, are you ready to write?'

109

(I was supposed to write an exam. A beautiful girl sat near me. I could not take my eyes off her. I could not write a word. After I came out I could write them.)

O sweet love! O great love!

You have feasted on me.

You have made me feel great.

You have my soul.

You are my life.

You are my light.

You are my everything.

You make me feel like I am nothing.

Your eyes are like two grapes

Which can be the sweetest the world has seen.

Your eyes reflect my spice.

Your eyes make me drunk forever.

Your nose is like a small shell

That no one would like to sell.

Your lips are like the petals

Of a heavenly garden.

Your hair is like a black stream

That makes my mind dream.

Did you put any cream

To make my heart scream?

Your eyebrows are so sharp

That they pierce into my heart.

God's masterpiece! Are you

His most favorite angel?

(I was only in the eighth standard then. I failed in that unit test but I
went to the ninth standard and remembered that incident.)

I know that beauty will fade with time.

Your face will shrink.

Your hair may fall.

But your heart and mind will always remain (mine!).

I will give a million to see you,

A billion to feel you,

A trillion for your smile

And my life for your love.

I will take you to heaven

When my loving heart stops.

I will damn myself

If my love ever stops.

(My friends were watching me write. They were peeping. I did not want them to tease me.)

I am sure you will be with me

Forever and forever.

I am sure you will love me

But what to do, you don't exist?

—Dominic Rodrigues

14/02/2003

110

ACT FIVE

Chorus

Has the author destroyed the character?

Or has the character destroyed the author?

Are they in love with each other?

Or are they still fighting?

Is this drama meaningful?

Or has the author stained it?

Can debate resolve our problems?

[Enter Dominic. Alone]

Dominic: Where are you? Are you hiding? I have nothing against you. Life is short just like the chapters in this novel. I do not believe in hating anyone. Please forgive and forget me. It is you who should say these words. I am happy with my life. The society can not do anything to change my mind. You are free to write a thousand novels about me. I just do not care. I just wish to ask a funny question—Are you trying to steal the title 'The Hero of the Novel' from me? [Smiles] You are so naughty. Come out! I know you are there.[Waits for some time. Smiles. Smiles again.] I am leaving. I have a family to take care of. [Leaves]

[Enter Novelist]

Novelist: He has changed. He is no longer a flat character. This is exactly what I wanted. I am also going to change. I am not stopping. Rebirths—2 will be out soon. It will also have life like short chapters that resembles movie shots. You can read my short novels like a movie. No, it will not be about Dominic. This drama is a tribute to the ancient Greek drama in its formative stages when there were only two characters on stage besides the chorus. My identity will remain a secret. I love this Dominic. I really love him. Chorus, have I answered you?

[Lights out.]

111

'Why don't you go out with friends and have fun?' said the psychologist.

'I will.' replied Dominic.

'If you have love in your heart just express it. Do you know how to express love?'

'Teach me. Will you?'

....

'What happened?'

'I am experiencing a writer's block. There is another problem too.'

'What is it?'

'It is also a block in my life.'

....

'Are you in love?'

'I don't know.'

....

'When I was young I wrote so many poems and short stories. I kept them very carefully. I showed it to one of my friends. He won a state level competition with it. He became my enemy. I started keeping away from friends. I was hiding things from them.'

....

'I am not coming to you again.'

'But why?'

'I am healed.'

'No, you are not.'

'Goodbye, Dr.Raguvaran.'

112

You would not be reading chapter 112 and 113 if you were not my best of friends.

I went to my dentist who promised me to do two root canal operations free—one tooth in the right and the other in the left. I sat in the comfortable dentist's chair and wanted to smile out of satisfaction of finishing my novel. The dentist put a syringe in my mouth. My lips were too numb to smile. The dentist with a mask put some kind of liquid into my mouth while his assistant vacuumed it out. A yellow light helped them to have a better look into my mouth. The yellow light was God who poured into my mind the wisdom of ages through Padmini, Immanuel, Abdullah and Dominic. Dear Reader, it is up to you to decide what you were in your past three births. It is I, the Novelist.

113

Dominic came home late with a smile on his face. He whispered to his wife about his new job as a schoolteacher. His wife was not that happy. She wanted her husband to be a rich man. She wanted to see him as a famous personality who is respected by everyone. The pure love that made her marry him was still there in her heart, but there was something missing.

Dominic was moving from room to room searching for something.

'What is it?' asked his wife.

'The autobiography I was writing is missing. I think I lost it when I took it along with my certificates to the interview. Oh! Putting it in my certificate file was a bad idea. Did you see it anywhere or did I put it somewhere else?'

'You said that you were not going to publish it, so why the anxiety?'

'I forgot to tell you something. I saw Shabri. I told you earlier that I was surprised to know that he is working as a clerk in a Bank. The Bank was on strike and whom do you think was leading this strike? It was Shabri. O! That guy!'

'You did not answer my question.'

Dominic who was very tired after the day's work went to sleep without replying to his wife's questions.

Dominic's wife took the autobiography, which she had secretly placed in her make-up box, and started reading it. She knew exactly what to do with it.

She visited Manju and her uncle Fr. Ben and discussed with them about Dominic. She went to Assisi College and did intensive research.

She declared, 'I am going to write the novel Dominic couldn't. I am going to be Dominic's alter ego. I am going to be Dominic's unconscious self. All his naughty thoughts and feelings are going to come out. I am going to play Freud. There is nothing left to be repressed. I am going to be Dominic's worst enemy. I am going to be Queen Shahrazad from the Arabian Nights who cooks up stories of male fantasy to protect herself from the vicious male ego. I am going to be the worst novelist.'

Fr. Ben and Manju, you are my best friends who are the only ones reading 112 and 113. Tell me if I have done anything wrong. I guess I have. Isn't male fantasy a good theme to write a novel on?

WARNING: Male fantasy works best when in remains in the realms of fantasy. It is only for internal use and not for external use. Its external use has caused all the evils in the world in the forms of war, violence and crime so far.

Epilogue

Sharticka, the head space scientist of planet Anue, stood before a great crowd to deliver his address; he had charisma. His dream of becoming the head of state was coming true. He spoke:

'Hail, the citizens of Anue!

Hail, The single country revolution!

Once we were divided into small countries that fought against each other for silly reasons. It was our late King Allke's idea to have the Planet Anue Army, PAA, through which we united all countries.

Hail PAA! I can say with pride in my heart that King Allke was my great-grandfather. Today we also salute our great astronauts who have come from a planet called Earth. They have proved to us something that we should be proud of . . .'

Hatis, who was one of the astronauts, was not listening. He thought about his wonderful mission to Earth. They had come to Earth searching for life. Sharticka had come up with the theory that life existed only on Planet Anue. He himself sent his astronauts along with some of his greatest rivals. Their ancestors strongly believed that there was life on the planet Earth. The name 'Earth' was coined by one of their ancestors who happened to visit Earth and had stayed there for a few years. When they reached Earth, life on it was destroyed. Everyone searched for the proof of life but no one could find any. The earthlings have destroyed themselves in such a way that no proof of their existence could be found. Hatis, who was dead sure that life had existed there found a DNA of an earthling and connected it into his brain. The DNA told his brain:

'I am Bavi. I have a confession to make. You do not have to believe me. A woman taught me a mantra. A simple beggar woman! Incidents that happened in my past three lives strayed into my mind. I did not believe in the concept of reincarnation before the incident. I, my soul, in its previous bodies made many mistakes. They also did very good things that went unnoticed. They were real heroes. I was a man called Dominic, who had a rare kind of personality that is not found today. The poems he wrote were stupid and immature. However, he was able to do a lot for the society. He wasted the first quarter of his life thinking about his instincts and passions without actually doing anything. He was able to make people happy. He was even ready to forgive a novelist who had written a stupid novel on him. Dominic's life along with the lives of two other women has taught me a great lesson in life. I look at my body that is burning with hunger, thirst and anger. I do not wish to live in a world in which people kill each other for a glass of water. I knew the meaning of life and did not wish to throw it away. I read about one of my ancestors in my palmtop who sold 5000000 laptops to buy the last apple fruit on earth. I feel ashamed of them. I feel ashamed of myself. A few years back I killed a man for my survival. I raped a woman a few months back. I robbed houses. So many years back these were called 'sins'. Only evil people do 'sins'. Today, everyone does it. The only sin known to man today is hunger. I have decided not to commit any sin again. I will not rob rape or kill again even if I die of hunger. For the first time in my life, my mind is going in the spiritual direction. I am thinking about God, a God who absent from our world today. I know the meaning of life. Thanks to the mantra! The divine wisdom is tickling from the inside.'

Hatis' fellow astronauts did not believe this because they thought this was impossible. Hatis brought before them many proofs but they were not ready to see them. They send a different report to the people of Anue. Hatis was thought to be a bit insane. He had secretly created a genetic programme to bring humankind back to life. He listened to the speech of Sharticka:

'One of our forefathers famously said, 'If you meet an alien talk to it in the language of music and mathematics.' There is no one to listen to our music. There is no one to understand our mathematics. We are alone— you and I. It is not that bad to be alone when you have a ruler to guide you, a savior to protect you and a God to bless you. As you all know,

I have bought the copyrights of all the folk-tales, prayers, songs, dance forms, religious texts, cultural rituals, flags, symbols and philosophies in this planet. I declare myself as the Emperor of the universe and the only living God. THERE NEVER WAS LIFE ON THE PLANET CALLED EARTH, THERE NEVER IS LIFE ON THE PLANET CALLED EARTH AND THERE NEVER WILL BE LIFE ON THE PLANET CALLED EARTH. Anue is the only planet in the entire universe that can be called ALIVE.'

Hatis wondered, 'Why do people fear the truth even when it is right before their eyes?'

—IT IS FINISHED—

THE NOVELIST'S AFTERWORD

Do not worry! Dominic is Ok, but I am not going to use 'The Novelist's Afterword' to answer to all questions like 'Which psychological disorder is the author suffering from?' I am going to use this session to tell you what my novel is about. Yes, you were wrong. Yes, you were right. You have the freedom to interpret my novel. Dominic has forgotten everything. He is having a happy married life.

My novel is not about the adventures of Dominic, nor is it about rebirth; my novel is not a postmodern work of art nor is it a novel at all. It is a long technical essay on the dual nature of light. The story is like light, it makes you to see something .Sometimes the story moves like particles and sometimes like waves. Just like a star, that is 10000 light years away, a culture a nation, a religion or a God can be 10000 story years away. The stories can be stupid, meaningless, coarse or vulgar (like my stories), but it can make people discover and grasp the subtlety of life. There is a story inside your mind, dear Readers, and that story shapes your life. Life is a story, a very long one, so many light years away. A story can be the light of your life; it can also be the darkness of your life. There is a period between day and night, between light and darkness. My novel is like the evening sky. Don't get pessimistic about its dark shades. Do not get carried away by the luminous sparkles that can put out the light and turn you blind.

Why did I write a novel? I wrote it to share my insights. My insights sparkle like the reflection of the setting sun on lakes that have already gone dark. They may be useless. They may resemble the flutters of a dying flame. They may be mediocre. But then, that is how life is. They may hurt. They may insult. They may empty your soul. But then, that is how you survive in this world. My words may die in your mind but their ghosts will haunt you. I am very sorry; we usually hurt the persons who we love the most. I love you, Dear Readers.

I have tried my best to hate my novel, but I could not (May be because I cannot hate life). Let every being on earth write novels and escape from each other. Then, who will sow the seed and who will make the world go round. The world is cool; it is because of us. We run about, do stupid things, talk nonsense, make love to ourselves and rock the world. The world is awesome because of you and me. If we can stop global warming and make the earth cooler; if we can stop all the wars and love each other; if we can accept differences; if we can tolerate the beliefs and feelings of others; if we can be happy and make others happy; what a happy world would it be! Our inner light will move as waves to every corner of the world. Do not worry! Aliens come to earth as in my epilogue only in the minds of sarcastic novelists.

Once there was a journalist who always wrote about scams, rapes, dirty politics, gruesome murders, and tragic deaths. He was very popular among people for his cynicism and his witty sarcasms on the futility of life. He got huge pay packages from the newspaper bosses. On a bright Sunday, he met a young boy who was reading one of his articles. He smiled at the boy but the boy did not smile back. 'You make me feel miserable,' said the boy, 'you take away the smiles from people and fill their heads with hate. You make people see the dark cloud on a bright sunny day.' The journalist tried to talk a lot about his profession and his work ethics but the boy was not ready to listen. The journalist started to write about the people who have changed the lives of others and make them happy. The journalist wrote about the sunny side of life and about spirituality. His popularity fell and his salary package was mediocre, but the young boy felt happy and the God from the above blessed him. I wish to write like the journalist. I do not know what is stopping me.

Once there was a boy, who used to scribble nonsensial words on the wall. He found joy in doing so. He also drew comical pictures and caricatures. When his father came home, he got angry and scolded him for ten minutes. Can I write with an innocence of a little boy? Dear Reader, will you be my father? When the little boy's mother came home, she saw her son crying. She comforted him and told him nice things about his nonsensial scribble. She gave him a blank paper and told him to write. The little boy smiled. Can I smile like the little boy? Dear Reader, will you be my mother? The little boy saw his sister drawing beautiful pictures and asked her, 'Will you teach me?' The little boy learned and became a great artist. Dear Reader will you be my sister?

Once an old lady hummed a tune into the ears of an infant girl. The infant had a sond sleep. The infant grew up into a beautiful woman and was lost in family politics. She was forced to marry and have a child. The child cried violently. She cried too. Slowly, from somewhere a beautiful tune came to her lips. The child stopped crying and a serene breeze blew into the invisible connection between the mother and the child. How did the woman remember the tune? All my words, thoughts and themes are as old as the tune of the old lady. I have borrowed them. One day it will be returned to the old lady. Was she God?

Once, a cloth maker spun five and a half meters of cloth to manufacture a blue sari. He made money. A woman imprinted leafy designs on it. She made money. A rich man bought it for his wife; he was forgiven for his lack of care. Time stole its brightness and the sari was gifted to a maid to hide a secret. The maid considered the sari to be a superior work of art. She used it to cover herself after being raped by her husband. It was later used as a cradle when the maid had a daughter. The maid's daughter used it in her school drama to symbolically represent a flowing river. My novel is like the blue sari. It is a victim of the society. Ideas are forced into it. It dances to the tunes of history. I am helplessly flowing like a river, an artificial river. Life awards me with experiences and I am forced to write.

This novel is about the modern human beings who have lost the confidence over their brains. His or her brain is only a footnote to the World Wide Web. We are run by laptops and mobile phones. Our deepest emotions go hiding between the bytes. We are eaten up and chewed. Some laptop somewhere is writing an anti-novel based on our lives. We are represented as liars, perverts and monsters. The real novel is stuck between our neurons. The fake one is spreading as gospel. Beware, dear Readers.

All people have their own brains, their own thoughts, feelings and opinions. Another person may find these thoughts unacceptable, unrealistic or offensive. Unfortunately, we have to live together as co-habitants of this wonderful earth. We need tolerance; we need patience. We need love; we need compassion. Tolerance is the charioteer of peace. If we all make tolerance our guide, we would not feel offended as Dominic. Dear Readers, thank you for tolerating me. The harmful words in this novel do not intend to harm anyone but to spread the light of tolerance all over the world. Using tolerance as my charioteer, I am spreading peace on this earth. The chariot is moving fast and it will continue to move.

I am a big fan of Freud's Psychoanalysis and the three rebirths represent Id, Ego and Super-ego. There are also other analogies.

Padmini's story—Id; Love; First stage of Dominic's marriage; Kama (the pleasures of the senses); Fire; Body.

Immanuel's story—Ego; Lust; Second stage of Dominic's marriage; Artha (the pleasures of materialism); Earth; Mind.

Abdulla's story—Super-ego; Passion; Third stage of Dominic's Marriage; Dharma (the pleasures of divine righteousness); Water; Soul.

Words can't be controlled by pen, philosophy or force. We do not write what we intend to write; we go beyond it. Can words change us? The question is obscure. All the words in this piece of fiction are purely lies. Hope you have enjoyed my lies.

ACT ZERO

[A desert. No actors or audience. Skeletons are used as puppets. No revenge, fight or love tunes are played. Desert]

Chorus:

We are sung up somewhere.

Don't persecute us.

We are experienced somewhere.

Don't believe us.

We are blinded somewhere.

Don't see with us.

We are starving somewhere.

Don't you feel like being with us.

When we cry, when we beg, all characters have gone silent.

When we struggle for love and life, no Novelist or Dominic are seen.

We pray looking into the heavens waiting for God to make Her visit.

We pray and wait for millions of years.

We can only hug each other and die.

Dead, we make love to the desert sand hoping to feed some life.

[No one listens to them; all are busy with their computers. God is seen from heaven coming down to rescue someone. Transparent white horses run towards the same direction. White papers and black papers dance in the air together.]

—IT IS NOT FINISHED—